Pushing Pause

Celeste O. Norfleet

Pushing Pause

KIMANI
TRU
™

PUSHING PAUSE

ISBN-13: 978-0-373-83085-5
ISBN-10:   0-373-83085-8

KIMANI TRU

FRESH. CURRENT. AND TRUE TO YOU.

Dear Reader,

What you're holding is very special. Something fresh, new and true to your unique experience as a young African-American! We are proud to introduce a new fiction imprint—Kimani TRU. You'll find Kimani TRU speaks to the triumphs, problems and concerns of today's black teens with candor, wit and realism. The stories are told from your perspective and in your own voice, and will spotlight young, emerging literary talent.

Kimani TRU will feature stories that are down-to-earth, yet empowering. Feel like an outsider? Afraid you'll never fit in, find your true love or have a boyfriend who accepts you for who you really are? Maybe you feel that your life is a disaster and your future is going nowhere. In Kimani TRU novels, discover the emotional issues that young blacks face every day. In one story, a young man struggles to get out of a neighborhood that holds little promise by attending a historically black college. In another, a young woman's life drastically changes when she goes to live with the father she has never known and his middle-class family in the suburbs.

With Kimani TRU, we are committed to providing a strong and unique voice that will appeal to *all* young readers! Our goal is to touch your heart, mind and soul, and give you a literary voice that reflects your creativity and your world.

Spread the word…Kimani TRU. True to you!

Linda Gill
General Manager
Kimani Press

KIMANI PRESS™

As always, to Fate & Fortune

Acknowledgments

To my teens, Jennifer and Christopher, who constantly remind me to let go of myself and enjoy life, and who encourage me to laugh, even when I don't feel like it. You are truly my heart. To my more-than-teens, Charles and Prince, it's great to know that you are always in my corner.

To my publisher, Linda Gill, thank you for developing Kimani TRU and for allowing me to participate in your dream.

To my editor, Evette Porter, much thanks for giving me the opportunity to write this book and for adding my voice to a wonderful program.

To my agent, Elaine English, thank you for your patience, positive advice and for always being in my corner.

CHAPTER 1

The Other Shoe

"You know when you have this strange feeling that something's up and you just can't shake it? Well, I've had that feeling for, like, a month now. It's weird. I'm waiting for the other shoe to drop but I haven't even heard the first one yet."
—*myspace.com*

ONE thing you need to know about me is that I don't do the status quo thing and for that reason, my mom and I argue, my dad and I argue, and my boyfriend and I argue, but one thing that's set in stone, I can count on them no matter what to always give me my way. You see, that's because bottom line is, it's all about me, Kenisha Lewis.

I'm cool and all, they say I'm spoiled, pampered, whatever, I'm just like my mom, but make no mistake, I handle my business. I love to dance and I dance everything, jazz, modern, tap, even a little ballet, but mostly I dance hiphop. Dance is the one thing in my life I can count on and I'm good, real good.

I go to Hazelhurst Academy for Girls in Northern Virginia. It's right across the bridge from D.C. so we can, like, look out the window and see the for real world. My school is all right, I guess. Seriously preppy, but that's okay sometimes. Right now it's summer, Tuesday, August-something, hot like somebody kicked open a furnace door and just left it.

So, up until a while ago my candy-ass life was perfect. At least that's what everybody thought from the outside looking in and I just let them think it 'cause up until then it was kind of true. It wasn't a never-ending extreme shopping spree or anything like that but I was seriously cultivating my significance. I had the perfect family, the perfect house, the perfect boyfriend and the perfect life. Until…

It was about five-thirty and I was getting ready to step out. My music, a Lil Mama *Lip Gloss* remix, was blasting at top volume 'cause I didn't want to hear it anymore, their muffled voices, the shrill cries, the deep confessions. I learned a long time ago to tune out, first with cartoons, then with television and then with my music.

"…so that's it, you just gonna walk out…"

"…we've been playing this thing over and over…"

I had no idea what they were arguing about, but whatever it was, it was serious. I only heard bits and pieces every now and then when they got really loud, but mostly I just tuned out.

"…this is my house and I'm not leaving…"

"…you don't have a choice…"

"…we'll see about that…"

"…take whatever, I don't care…"

That one started an hour ago. They fought so loud, it sounded like World War III had jumped off up in there, friggin' scud missiles and nuclear bombs and all. My mom and dad are a gen-u-wine trip like that. They always got something going on, but lately it's been worse than ever. He walked out two weeks ago with his bags in his hands. I knew that something was up with them, but neither was talking. When I called my dad at his office and asked him, he was, like, ask your mom. And when I asked, my mom was, like, nothing. But something was definitely up.

"…you and that bitch can think again, you hear me…"

"…bullshit, this is a long time coming, you know it, here, take this…"

"…what's this, what am I supposed to do with this…"

"…read it, it explains everything…"

So tonight he stopped by and they got into it again. It's always about the same thing, my dad stepping out. He's fiftysomething, old as hell and still frontin', thinking he's a player. He used to be a professional football player, but now he's owns a computer software business and, like, fifteen years ago they developed this new software program, then sold it for big bucks.

"…screw you and your other women…"

"…you don't have a choice, my attorney…"

So now he's got deep pockets and those stupid skanks at his office flock to him like flies to new crap. It pisses my mom off and I don't know why he does that, 'cause he knows that my mom is going off on his ass. She seriously needs to control her man. Thank God I don't have her issues.

"...a piece of paper don't mean shit to me..."

"...this is no joke, I'm serious, it's over..."

"...you think you can do this to me, you can try..."

It went on like that for a while, then I heard the inevitable slap and then a scuffle. My mom's a slapper. She'll reach up and slap somebody's face in a second. I remember we were out to dinner one time and my dad turned to check this big-boob, big-butt waitress out and just as he turned back around, my mom was there meeting him with the flat of her hand across his face. The crack echoed all over the restaurant.

Everybody turned to see what he was gonna do. As usual my dad played it off like it was nothing. He joked and laughed, lightening the mood, but I knew he had to be seriously embarrassed. He's, like, six-feet-four and all muscle at about two hundred and thirty pounds. And if he were to ever hit her back, he'd seriously knock her into next week.

Mom knew that. She took great pleasure in hitting my dad, knowing that he'd never hit her back. He'd hold her and back her away, but he would never lay a hand on her.

"...if you think you and that bitch..."

"...you need to bump all that poor-me drama, you knew this was coming for the last fifteen years..."

My cell vibrated in my pocket, so I went into my bathroom and answered 'cause the music was still blasting.

"Kenisha, girl, you ready yet or what?" Chili asked.

Chili Rodriguez is my girl. She moved to the neighborhood a few years ago, but we just started hanging out recently, when she started attending Hazelhurst Academy.

"No, not yet," I told her, looking at a stupid pimple that decided to just pop up this afternoon.

"Well, hurry up, I don't want to be late. You know that place is small as hell and it's gonna be packed in there and we still have to catch the Metro into the city." Chili's Honduran and her accent is really thick, so when she's excited, I can barely understand her.

"A'ight, gimme twenty minutes."

"You better be ready, 'cause I ain't waiting all night for your ass."

"A'ight," I said, then closed my cell. Sometimes my girl Chili really pisses me off. She thinks she's hot stuff since her dad blew up large and dumped serious presidents on a BMW for her sixteenth birthday last June.

"…just go, get out, I don't give a shit, leave…"

"…I'm sick of your drama…"

Okay, enough already. I went back into the bedroom and figured that they're in the hallway now 'cause I can hear them clearly. I love my parents, but they just don't get it. They need to chill with all this drama.

So I'm named after my dad, Kenneth. They wanted a boy, expected a boy, but they got me instead. Surprise! My mom's name is Barbra. She's a young thirty-four and a serious computer geek. She had me when she was nineteen and working in my dad's office. She's usually okay, but lately she's been seriously nuts, popping pills like Tic-Tacs.

My dad is sixteen years older than her. "That's my Barbie doll," he always says, because she's so pretty and petite and still has a slamming body. I guess that would make me Stacy or Skipper or whatever unexplained Mattel baby doll showed up after them.

My mom's about a hundred and twenty pounds now, thanks to her diet pills, but her weight goes up and down all the time. She's five-foot-two with long good hair and skin the color of burnished copper. My dad is the exact opposite, he's got kinky hair, a wide nose, but he's real light-skinned 'cause his mom is white, but we never talk about her 'cause she walked out and left him after his dad died. I have no idea what that was all about and nobody talks about it, so it just hangs there.

Anyway, I guess I'm in the middle someplace. I got a mix of my mom and my dad's complexions, my mom's hair and everybody said I look like her, just taller, like my dad.

So getting back to the fight, it was going on for a while, but now it's been quiet for about ten minutes, then I heard the front door slam.

"Kenisha, turn that damn music down. Kenisha!"

Dammit. I knew this was gonna happen, stuff like this always happens when they fight, I get stuck in the middle. So now since he walked out in the middle of the fight, she turns to me and it's my turn to navigate this drama and deal with her crap, acting like it's all about my drama, please. The only reason she even came in my room is that she needs to use me to get back with him, same game every time. I plug my MP3 earbuds in my ears and turn my back.

So now she's standing in the doorway talking to me, but with the loud music and my earbuds on I'm trying to ignore her.

"Kenisha, do you hear me talking to you?" she said with her fist balled on her hip while still standing in the doorway to my bedroom.

So I looked up and removed my earplugs. I picked up the remote and turned the music off. "I hear you," I said calmly, knowing that my mom hates it when I act calmer than her, particularly when she's all pissed off and out of control. I can tell she's been drinking her Veuve Clicquot or her Opus One and taking her Vicodin, Zoloft or Lustral, whichever. She always takes pills after a fight with my dad. Antidepressants, they're supposed to help her to calm down.

"Change your clothes and cover that thing up. I told you not to get it, but you just don't listen." She started in on me again, her words slightly slurred as she spoke. "And you go right out and do it anyway, then you wind up in the emergency room half the night and you think you're just going to walk out of here looking like that, like nothing's wrong. I don't think so. I told you you're grounded, no dance class and no hanging out with that boy."

"I don't know why you hatin' on LaVon, he ain't do nothing to you."

"He's a football player, isn't he?"

"No, he plays basketball."

"Same thing."

"It is not."

"Close enough, now keep that music down, you're in for the night." She turned, paused, then turned back to continue.

"And being boy-crazy won't get you anywhere in this

world, believe me. You can't sacrifice your dreams and your future for anyone."

"I'm not boy-crazy and if you're referring to LaVon…"

"You know he only wants one thing from you. He's got his hormones on overdrive and I don't want you messing up your life for him and his urges."

"I'm not," I said. I don't know why she needs to go there. "LaVon and I talked about sex, but I'm not ready and he's cool with it."

"If he starts pressuring you…"

"He hasn't, he doesn't, he won't," I lied, knowing that was all he wanted to do and that was all he ever talked about. "You always think that I'm doing something, I'm not and besides, he won't even be there tonight. He's going on some college tour with his father today."

"Uh-huh, still, I said you're not going."

"Dad already said I could go," I said defiantly.

"I don't give a crap what he said and don't play that mess with me," she said, slicing her perfectly manicured finger through the air fiercely. I could see the anger spike again. "I know damn well he didn't say that you could go all the way to D.C. at some six o'clock at night for some three-hour recital. You're fifteen years old, no," she said, ending the conversation and walking back down the hall to her bedroom.

I went to my bedroom door. "It's not a recital, it's a video taping and it's at Freeman Dance Studio with Gayle Harmon and her steppers, she choreographs all the hip-hop video moves. She's good and she's on TV all the time doing hip-hop."

My mom stopped midway down the hall and turned to me. "I don't care if she's on the moon all the time, you're not going and that's final. And I don't want you around that video crap, shaking your behind half-naked like you don't know any better." She turned and kept walking.

I stood in the doorway considering my options. I could go with the "dad said I could" line again, but that might just piss her off more, so I rely on the old standard then follow her into her bedroom. "Fine, but I have their tickets, what am I supposed to do?"

"You have whose tickets?" she asked.

"Chili and Jalisa's," I said, lying my butt off, of course.

"Call them; tell them you're not going. They can come over and pick up the tickets."

I looked at my watch for added convincing. "They're already on the way, we're supposed to meet there in an hour, and I'm already late." She glared at me and I smiled inwardly 'cause I know that look. She's pissed off, but there was no way she was gonna let me not go now. My friends are her friends' kids and there was no way she was gonna be embarrassed like that. Appearance is everything to her. I looked up innocently, waiting for it to come. It did. "You'd better bring your narrow behind straight home afterwards, do you hear me?"

I nodded. But we both knew that was not gonna happen.

CHAPTER 2

When Life Is Good

"So we run around all our lives looking for something to make us happy, when all along what we're looking for is right inside us, all we have to do is be still and push pause and let it come."

—*myspace.com*

Freeman Dance Studio was our place.

Jalisa Saunders, my best friend, and I have been taking classes there nearly all our lives and we hang out there at least three times a week. We met eleven years ago when our moms brought us there on the same day. We were four years old and have been best friends ever since. So this place is like a part of us, and at fifteen we were just about teaching the classes.

We know tap and ballet and modern and jazz, but it was hip-hop that was the best. We thrived on it, the sounds, the beats, the rhythms, the clothes, the movements, the people. That's 'cause it's our generation and it belongs to us and sure-nuff tonight's performance proved it.

I can still hear the music in my head, so I was bumping and popping my neck and shoulders to the beat, 'cause for the first time in a long time I felt free. This was my world and I was seriously feeling it.

"I can't wait to get back to dance class after this stupid punishment, that was seriously hot," I said to my girls Chili and Jalisa as we walked down the long hall past the reception area, offices and dance studios towards the exit. The three of us are tight but we didn't always used to be. It used to be me, Jalisa and Diamond, but Diamond started acting all weird and stuck-up, so now it's Chili and we do almost everything together.

"It was too hot," Chili agreed, then crinkled her nose as someone pushed past her, almost knocking her off her spiked heels. "Hey, watch it, damn, that's why I hate coming down here to this place. They should have taped the video somewhere else 'cause this place is totally trashed."

"But it's our home," I said proudly, "so you need to recognize."

"That is sure-nuff right, my sistah girl," Jalisa said as we slapped hands. Chili sucked her teeth as we laughed. "And my girl, Gayle, was too hot," Jalisa added, joining in on my impromptu dance, mimicking my movements exactly as Chili watched us and started clapping. We laughed like we always do when we start doing our thing in public.

"Definitely, did you see how that one dancer jumped up, then dropped and did that little spin, then got back up? That was too hot," Chili added, but we could barely understand her as usual, 'cause she was excited and her accent is seriously thick.

"What in the world did you just say?" Jalisa asked jokingly. "Girl, you need to speak English, you in America now, Toby."

I bust out laughing, then Jalisa joined in. She'd been doing the Kunta Kinte thing from the movie *Roots* ever since we stayed up all night at my house and watched every episode from start to finish a few weeks ago.

"Y'all ain't funny, that shit's not funny," Chili said, getting pissed like always when we joked around about her accent. "So you just need to stop that *Roots* shit. I'm tired of hearing it. Don't nobody care less about that slave shit no more. And I'm tired of hearing it and I'm tired of you making fun of me when I talk. My mom and dad are rich and my *papi* can buy and sell both of your asses in a minute," she said, then snapped her finger to make her point.

With the thick accent again plus the reference to buying and selling us made me and Jalisa burst out laughing all over again. Chili didn't get it, so she just rolled her eyes. It was Chili's thing to throw her family's newfound wealth at everybody when she got pissed. Unfortunately for her, nobody really cared.

When her parents first got here, they tapped into the Latino housing and food service market and now they made big bucks. Nobody really cared one way or the other, but since she didn't have any other power to throw around, she went with the "I have more money than you" taunt. Childish, I know, but whatever.

"Chill out, girl, you know we're just messing with you," I said to her.

"Yeah, you know we girls," Jalisa added, reaching out to hug her as she slapped her arm away and stepped aside, still acting like she was mad at us.

"That's right," I said, blocking her on the other side.

Sandwiched between us, she had no recourse but to give in. "Yeah, right, but y'all two play too much," Chili said, finally relenting, but still keeping her bottom lip poked out as we all three continued walking.

"Check it out," Jalisa said, trying to repeat the action, spinning around on the ball of her foot, then stopping, just as the performer did.

We continued joking and laughing as the doors to the Freeman Dance Studio opened wide and a steady flow of hip-hop wannabes streamed out.

Everybody was pumped and still having a great time, especially me. I was right up there with them, on a dancer's high. Four and a half steady hours of hip-hop, old-school and jazz nearly tore the roof off the hundred-and-sixty-year-old building we called our home away from home.

The studio was named for the intersection of three streets coming together. It was called Freeman's Point. History has it that a congregation of freed slaves was killed in this spot during an abolitionist march about a hundred and fifty years ago. The building, now dilapidated with no heat in the winter and no air in the summer, was a wreck, but nobody cared 'cause Gayle Harmon and her steppers brought it, then seriously kicked it out. Of course, shooting a video for Tyrece didn't hurt, either.

Tyrece, aka T.G., is actually Tyrece Grant, a guy from around the way who had made it out. There were two popular versions to his story. One had him as a gang banger and gun dealer who'd gone to the penitentiary for a double murder, then got off on a legal technicality. The other was that he was a full-scholarship Cornell University student who was discovered doing his thing onstage in a college talent show, then dropped out to become a star.

Either way he was now hip-hop royalty and as such deserved his props. Tonight he'd chosen to bring his court to the Freeman Dance Studio.

The music was loud and bumping, the place was packed and everybody within a mile and a half was still jamming. We weren't in the video exactly, but whatever, you never can tell. Being in the crowd, maybe, why not, we could be.

"Aw, check, you never guess what I heard," Chili said excitedly as we continued down the street.

"What?" I asked, still pumped up.

"Tyrece is going over to Giorgio's Pizza Palace to celebrate the video wrap."

"No way," I said cynically. "Why would he celebrate at a corner pizza parlor?"

"It used to be his hangout in the day, so he's going back to check it out and bring some of his boys with him."

"No way," I repeated.

"When?" Jalisa said, ignoring me.

"Tonight, now," Chili said animatedly.

"Get out," I contended, still finding it hard to believe.

"Seriously," Chili insisted.

"Check, I'm going," Jalisa said.

"Me, too," Chili added needlessly.

They stopped walking and looked at me. I looked at my cell phone. The supposedly two-hour show had gone on for four and a half hours. "I gotta get home," I said, knowing I'd have to hear it when I got home. The last thing I needed was more drama, particularly after my mom had just argued with my dad.

"Aw, come on, Kenisha, you're already grounded for the piercing thing, what's the worst that can happen?" Chili said.

"Hey, yo, y'all going over to the pizza place to hang? We heard Tyrece is stopping by later with some of his crew," somebody said to us as they passed by.

"Sure-nuff," Chili said before anyone else could answer.

"We are?" I asked. At fifteen, I know my own mind and I don't usually follow just anybody, so when the crowd is going one way, I usually make it a point to go the opposite or at least make up my own mind. But Chili and Jalisa are different. They're my girls and all, but sometimes they be seriously trippin'. "Y'all don't seriously think Tyrece is gonna hang out some old pizza parlor, do you?"

"Yeah," Chili said indignantly, then turned to me. "Don't tell me you're seriously gonna miss tonight, damn, Kenisha! You've been going to the place since forever and now that they're gonna party at your spot, you want to miss it? Are you out of your mind?"

"Yeah, I'm out of my mind," I said, agreeing, "plus it's late and I'm tired."

"I'm not," Chili said adamantly, "and there is no way I'm missing the hottest throw-down this town has seen all summer."

"Do you seriously think Tyrece is gonna show up at some greasy pizza place that serves sweet tea and not some top-shelf champagne?"

"Why not?" she asked. "Didn't he, like, grow up around here or something? It would be like coming home."

"Oh, please," I said as we came to the corner. We stopped and looked in two different directions. We could either keep straight one block and go to the pizza place or turn and head for the Metro back to Virginia.

"Pizza place," Chili said.

"Home," I said.

So as usual Chili and I looked at Jalisa to settle the dispute. "Would y'all please leave me out of your drama?"

"Come on, Jalisa," Chili whined in that way that she did.

Jalisa looked at us, then at her watch. "Okay, since we already missed our train and the next one isn't for another fifty minutes, we'll hang for thirty minutes tops," Jalisa said, then turned to me. "But if nothing's going on, we'll leave earlier, deal?"

"Deal," Chili said, obviously confident that the place would be jumping and we'd be there all night.

I half nodded, knowing that we'd be there at least forty-five minutes. "Fine, thirty minutes and then we're out."

Chili nodded. "Fine, so it's settled."

"Yo, Kenisha, where the party at?" someone called out from behind us.

We turn around and see Jerome Tyler, aka Li'l T, and some of his friends walking behind us. They're a trip 'cause they act all hard and everything, but really they are just a bunch of eighth graders trying to hang.

"Isn't it past your bedtime Li'l youngin?" Chili said, knowing he'd hear her. She's always talking down to Li'l T 'cause he's had a crush on her since the first time he laid eyes on her. He introduced himself by grabbing her butt and running, so he's been trying to kiss her ass ever since.

The insult hit hard as usual, so his boys started laughing and crackin' on him, so of course he had to respond.

"What, you offering your bed, shorty? That's cool, I'll polish your little Chili pepper real good," he snapped back, then stuck out his tongue and started making sucking sounds, causing his boys to hoot and holler. They slapped and shook his hand in congrats.

"He gets on my nerves," Chili said to us as we kept walking.

"Yo, Kenisha, hook a brotha up, where it's at, where the party at?"

"Y'all know you too young to be hanging out this late," Jalisa joined in.

"Who you calling young, I'll show you young," one of his boys answered, then grabbed the crotch of his low-riding baggy jeans and came up behind Jalisa acting like he was gonna grind on her butt.

I turned around and he stopped, causing a new round of cracks on him for punking out.

"Yo, Kenisha," Li'l T said, drawing my attention away from his friend. "Check this out." He started dancing, trying to do some of the steps he'd seen the performers do earlier. His MP3 player was wired to his earbuds as he jerked his neck, popped his head and arms, then moved his shoulders like a tidal wave getting shock treatments. In a seamless flow of pop-and-lock moves, he started sliding and snapping his legs as his feet spun in circles in perpetual motion. I had to admit he was looking pretty good with mad skills, for about a minute and a half.

Chili and Jalisa had turned around by this time and we were all clapping and cheering him on as a semicircle began to form around him. One of his friends joined in, then another and another, and they each started to do different steps and they were really starting to look hot.

Then one of his friends stumbled and tripped and fell off the pavement bumping into a parked car, which set the alarm off, then someone in the house across the street started yelling. So of course we all broke up laughing and ran like hell.

"You need to stop showing off, little boy, before you hurt something," Jalisa said, seeing Li'l T as he shook hands with his friends. We laughed again. Li'l T was always trying to show off for Chili, and of course she did her best to ignore him.

"I know they're not even trying to be following us," Chili said when she turned around and saw Li'l T and his friends still walking behind us.

"They're probably just going to the pizza place, too," I said, knowing that Li'l T would walk into hell if it meant getting Chili's attention. "You know they go there after dance class as much as we do."

Li'l T was tall and lean with a soft, dark-chocolate complexion and bright white teeth and an always-ready smile that seemed to brighten even more when Chili was around. He was in the eighth grade, middle school, and as far away from us as light was from dark. High school made all the difference: as far as we were concerned, he was a kid.

Usually we allowed him to hang, but tonight we ignored him 'cause we were seriously hot. We looked it and we acted it. Although Chili must have skipped the casual but cool memo 'cause she was sporting a two-sizes-too-small midriff top, a micro-miniskirt and wearing four-inch stilettos, looking like she just got finished working the brass pole in a strip club. She usually dresses fifteen minutes from being a stripper, but tonight she was dressed ten minutes from actually selling it on the street. No joke, she looked whacked, but we didn't say anything 'cause getting noticed was seriously her thing.

Jalisa, sans her usual microbraids and optioning instead for flatiron-straight curls, wore wide-legged dance sweats with a tight, sleeveless tank top under a hot pink Guess hoodie with a dozen or so silver bangles on her wrists. I had on my Baby Phat baggy sweatpants with the matching tight-fitted sweatsuit hoodie zipped halfway down the front.

Anyway, as we approached the pizza place, we could see that it was already jam-packed. There were people hanging outside dancing and playing, talking and joking around 'cause mostly everybody else was inside.

CHAPTER 3

Time to Go Now

"There's nothing like being alone in a crowded room hearing yourself breathe for the first time."
—*myspace.com*

The overhead sign light was on and the place was lit up, but there were so many people that it looked dark inside.

"Wow, check this out, there's no way we're gonna get a seat in there," I said, surprised by the crowd so thick that it continued overflowing out onto the sidewalk.

"We should have left the dance studio earlier," Chili said. "You're right, we're never going to get in there."

"Don't worry, Diamond is saving us a seat," Jalisa said. We both looked at her like she was crazy. "Don't start," Jalisa said, knowing exactly what we were thinking. Diamond was one of her friends, not ours, and she knew we didn't like her.

Before, it was the three of us that used to be tight, me, Jalisa and Diamond, but that was before she changed. I don't know what happened to her. Now we don't trust her anymore. Nobody does anymore.

Diamond stepped to Chili's boyfriend right there at Chili's sweet sixteen birthday party, got caught right in the act, then tried to play it off like it wasn't her fault. And now the thing was Chili told me that Diamond was tripping after LaVon and I wasn't having it.

LaVon and I have been together since eighth grade. We had our future all planned, high school, college, grad school, then marriage, but then two summers ago he grew almost two feet and every basketball coach in the area was after him and even though they weren't supposed to, college coaches and recruiters were hot on him, as well, and so was every twitching hot-ass, including my used-to-be-best friend, Diamond Riggs.

"Come on, let's just go in," Jalisa said insistently, pulling my arm.

So we went inside. Jalisa was looking around for Diamond. We walked around the whole place, cruising the crowd, then stopped by the front door again.

"Let's just find a spot to stand and look around instead of walking all over the place," I said.

"Maybe your friend ain't show up," Chili said in a catty way.

"Good, then we can go," I said.

"There she is by the back door," Jalisa said, pointing.

We walked over to where she was sitting and saw her talking to… "LaVon?" I said.

He looked up and saw me standing there and smiled like he wasn't caught. "Hey, K-shorty, what's up?" he asked innocently, using his nickname for me like I was blind or something.

"Nothing," I said. "What's up with you, you hanging out now or what? I thought you said you were doing colleges all week."

"Nah, I had to check out early. There was nothing happening with the college thing, so I decided to step out with my boys."

"Uh-huh," I said, then looked at Diamond as she smiled tightly.

"Hey," she said generally to the three of us.

"Girl, did you check that out tonight, it was too hot. Tyrece is too fine. I can't wait to check him when he gets here," Jalisa said as she sat down on the empty stool on the other side of Diamond.

"Nah, I missed it. I came straight here," Diamond said, knowing that I was gritting on her, so she made sure not to look in my direction.

"Where's Isaac?" Jalisa asked LaVon, looking around for his best friend. She had a serious crush on him.

"He's over there," LaVon said to Jalisa as he unfolded his six-foot-three frame to stand. "Come on." He took my hand, pulled me in and kissed me on the lips as we started to move through the crowd. I turned seeing Diamond staring and I smiled. I wasn't gonna make it that easy for her. Possession was nine-tenths of the law and she had better recognize that.

So we walked over and talked to Isaac and some other friends for a while. His boys were there and we were all talking, but I was still pissed. I still couldn't believe that

Diamond was all up in LaVon's face like that. If he wasn't on his way to the NBA, half the girls wouldn't even give him the time of day.

So now he was holding on to me, but I was tired of his crap, too. So I went to the bathroom just to chill a minute. As soon as I walked in, some girl came over to me.

"Hey, I saw you outside, do you know Jade Dawson?"

"Yeah," I said.

"I'm Leelah, Jade and I graduated last year. She's cool, we had a few classes together. I thought she said she had a sister in dance, too, you look just like her."

"I'm Kenisha, Jade's my cousin."

"Did you check her out tonight? Girlfriend was tight up there, and her moves were too fierce."

"You Jade's cousin?" someone asked. I nodded.

"Yo, tell Jade that Denise says hey," someone else added behind me.

"I didn't know she was still hanging with Tyrece. She looked hot up there."

"Yeah, she did," I said, having no idea that my cousin was so popular around there. So I'm standing at the sink, talking, and Diamond came in.

Always perfect, she had on her Air Force One sneakers, skintight low-riding hip-hugging Hilfiger dance jeans with a snug-fit midriff top that choked everything in place.

So she stood across the room and started grittin' on me like she wanted to start something.

"What, you think you want to say something to me?" I asked her boldly in a threatening tone. The girls I was with stopped to check out what was about to go on.

"Look, you think I want LaVon, I don't. You know we all go way back and I know he's your man so you can chill on that 'cause he came over to talk to me. So if you can't hold on to him, then that is your drama, not mine," she said, obviously nervous.

The remark was intended to sting, but it fell off like cheap jewelry. 'Course I wasn't having that. There was no way I was gonna let her front on me like that in front of these people. "I know you ain't frontin' on me, 'cause you don't even know me anymore," I said, then Leelah, the girl I was just talking to, stepped up and put her hands on her hips, obviously ready to get busy if anything jumped off. Then a couple of her girlfriends stepped up, too.

Diamond looked at the girls around me and glared. "I'm just saying, it wasn't me, so you need to check your man and your other friend..."

"Whatever," I said dismissively just as Chili walked in, and several of the other girls in the bathroom started checking us out, too. But I was cool, I wasn't about to be rolling around on the bathroom floor fighting over LaVon Oliver. But Diamond kept staring like she wanted to say more. I looked at her and cocked my head. "So, what, is that all you got?" I asked.

She glared at Chili.

"What up?" Chili said as she walked over and stood by my side, looking at Diamond.

Diamond looked her up and down but didn't say anything. "Ask her," I said as the bathroom got completely quiet and still 'cause everybody was waiting to see what was going to happen. Everybody turned to stare at Diamond.

"Ain't nothing up, Chili," Diamond said finally, then walked out of the bathroom.

"What was all that about?" Chili asked me.

I just shook my head. The whole thing was pathetic. If Diamond thought that I was gonna fight her over LaVon, she needed to check herself. "What is her problem?" I said.

"Jealously is a terrible thing," Chili said, then turned to the mirror to reapply her lip balm.

I went back out, and big surprise, a fight broke out between these two guys, but it was quickly squashed. The bathrooms emptied and I saw Chili across the room. Her hormones were on serious overdrive as usual. She was hooked up in a corner sucking face with some guy I know she knew nothing about. She's got serious issues when it comes to hooking up.

Jalisa and I are a bit more selective.

Personally, I don't give anything away, which is why LaVon was giving me drama. He was on my case 24/7 'cause his boys found out that we weren't kickin' it and he's not getting any. He was stressing, but he'll get over it, he always does.

So I'm sitting there checking out the place and it's like Penn Hall High School let out. That's cool and all, mostly because we don't really deal with Penn Hall.

So my Chris Brown ringtone sounds and I looked down at my cell to check out the caller ID. It's my mom calling again. She was seriously trippin' as usual. Don't get me wrong, I love my mom and my dad and I love my life. I love everything about it, well, mostly. My mom is cool and all, but sometimes she can be so closed-minded about my life. My cell vibrates again, it's my mom, of course, and I ignore it.

By the time we left, it was way after twelve o'clock. Tyrece never did show, like that was ever really gonna happen.

CHAPTER 4

Getting Home from the Other Side

"Devoid of air, we die a little bit at a time. We gasp and choke and hold on to every precious morsel we can get. But in the end, the joke is we still die."

—*myspace.com*

"COME on, Kenisha, run!" Jalisa yelled.

"I'm coming," I sputtered, laboring hard to control my breathing while feeling slightly light-headed.

"We're gonna miss it," Chili said.

"No, we're not, hurry up," Jalisa called out as she jogged to the top of the steps and looked back at Chili right behind her and me bringing up the rear.

"Y'all go ahead, I'm coming," I called out.

Chili brushed past Jalisa and headed for the platform, then turned. "The train's coming!" she yelled. "The lights are blinking on the platform, hurry up."

"Go ahead, I'm right behind you."

"No," Jalisa said firmly, waiting for me. "You know the rule, we stay together no matter what."

She was right. It was a promise Jalisa, Diamond and I made a long time ago when we were kids. We took an oath and everything. We were always going to be friends and stick together, no matter what. So much for oaths.

A prerecorded announcement sounded. This was the last train to Virginia. If we don't catch this one, we'll have to find another way home. That meant calling one of our parents, and neither one of us wanted that.

"It's the last train," Jalisa said just as I met her at the top of the steps. We turned to seeing Chili waving frantically. The train was just speeding by, blowing her long, riotous, corkscrew curls across her face. "Come on," she called but was drowned out by the train's deafening arrival. She ran to the last car, then to the closest door. When it opened, she stood midway blocking the doors from closing again. "Come on."

Jalisa and I ran down the platform toward the train just as the inside lights blinked and the door-closing warning beeps sound. We ran faster seeing Chili's alarmed expression.

As we ran I saw the conductor poke his head out the front window of the first car, obviously hearing our yells and seeing that someone was blocking the door from closing. Chili stood firm as we reached the door. As soon as Jalisa and I were on board, she stepped away and the door immediately closed.

Hanging on to the poles in the center, breathless and exhausted, we busted out laughing as the train slowly pulled out. "I can't believe we did that," Jalisa said in short gasps, coughing and sputtering. The three-block run from the pizza parlor to the Metro station had us all panting breathlessly.

"We should join the track team after that sprint," Chili said, also coughing and laughing.

I nodded but didn't respond. My head was spinning in circles, and an elephant was sitting on my chest. Breathing was getting more and more difficult. I bent over, coughing and holding my chest.

I heard Jalisa stop laughing. She must have noticed my difficulty. "Kenisha, you okay?" she asked me, concerned.

Chili stopped laughing, too, then knelt down and placed her hand on my back. "Come on, you need to sit down," she said.

"No...I'm...fine," I said then looked up and nodded my head. "I...just...need...to...catch...my...breath," I said haltingly, holding my hand up to my chest, coughing, as we stood around the center pole. I have asthma attacks sometimes when I overdo it. I've had it since I was a kid, and every once in a while I wound up in the hospital because of it.

"You have your inhaler?" Jalisa asked. I nodded as she put her arm around me, closing in as we always did when one of us was in trouble. I started digging in my small shoulder bag and pulled out my inhaler and I opened my mouth and pressed the button, then inhaled deeply. A quick blast of medication streamed down into my lungs.

The dizzying feeling returned, but I could feel my lungs starting to open immediately. I closed my eyes, waiting, knowing that Chili and Jalisa were also waiting for the reaction. Either I'd be okay or not. A few minutes passed and I began to breathe better. Slow and steadily, I took deep lung-filling gasps of air. Relieved, I was back. I looked up and saw the concern on Chili and Jalisa's faces, I smiled and nodded and we started laughing all over again.

"Girl, you better stop scaring us like that," Chili said, playfully slapping my arm.

"I'm serious," Jalisa said, still looking concerned, "you almost gave me a heart attack."

"I'm fine," I said, "I guess I just overdid it tonight."

"Are you sure?"

"Yeah, I'm sure."

The conversation instantly changed and we were back to talking about the video taping and the dancers, then we went on to talk about the pizza parlor afterwards. LaVon and Diamond came up, but we dissed the conversation quickly and went on to something else.

"I'm glad we went even if Tyrece didn't show up," Chili said happily.

"Me, too," Jalisa said.

By the time the train pulled into the last station I felt fine. We got off laughing, talking and joking around. We walked through the dark Metro station to Chili's car, parked under the streetlight in the near empty lot.

Still laughing and joking, we piled in, me up front and Jalisa in the back. Chili started it up, but nothing happened. She tried again and it started. We pulled out of the parking space, then drove halfway out of the lot when the car stalled. We drifted to the side into another parking space, closer to the exit. Jalisa and I watched as

Chili started it again, then two seconds later it died again. She tried it again, but this time it wouldn't start at all. She tried it again, and still nothing happened.

"What's wrong with it?" Jalisa asked from the back-seat.

"I don't know, it's always weird," Chili answered.

"Try it again," I said hopefully, looking at the illumi-nated clock on the dash panel.

She tried one more time then looked at the gas meter. "Oh, crap, I forgot to get gas today, I think it's on empty again."

"Again?" I said. You don't know how many times I'd gotten stuck in the street with Chili because she forgot to put gas in the car, even when she was borrowing her mother's car. It happened all the time. Getting a BMW for her sixteenth birthday was seriously on time, but Chili was the only person I knew who couldn't seem to get that whole fuel-goes-into-car-to-make-it-run thing. If her father didn't fill up her tank every other day, it would never get done.

Now the three of us were sitting there, looking at the little red arrow, willing it to move, but of course it didn't. So it was late and we were sitting in a deserted Metro parking lot in the middle of the night with no way to get home.

"What are we gonna do now?" Jalisa asked, sitting back.

"You have to call your mom," Chili said to me.

"Don't even try it, I'm sneaking in, remember?" I said.

"Come on, it's not like she don't know you're out."

"That's not the point, if she's asleep, I'm not about to be calling and waking her up."

"What about your dad, is he still away on business?"

"Yeah, he's still away," I lied.

"All right, Jalisa, it's you," Chili said decisively, looking in the rearview mirror, "you gotta call your mom."

"No way, I'm not waking her up at one o'clock in the morning. She'll kill me if she knows I was out this late past my curfew. I'll be grounded for life. Can't you call your mom or your dad?"

"They're not home," Chili said.

Big surprise there, I thought to myself but didn't say anything. We sat for a while, thinking. "Jalisa, can you call Natalie?" I asked hopefully, turning around to her.

"Yeah, call Natalie, she's cool, she'll cover for us," Chili agreed quickly.

Jalisa rolled her eyes. "Can't we just call a cab?"

"And wait forever, hell, no, come on, Jalisa, just call Natalie," Chili said. "Seriously, we don't have a choice."

Jalisa looked at me and I nodded. We both knew that we didn't have a choice. "Natalie will probably get on our case a little and complain, but she'll still be cool. She's always cool."

"Yeah, right, she's gonna kill me, too," Jalisa said as she pulled out her cell phone and dialed the phone number to the nurses' station at the hospital.

I always envied Jalisa and her sister. And even though Jalisa used to tell me how much they argued and complained that Natalie always got on her nerves, I knew that they were still seriously tight. Whenever Jalisa got in trouble with their mom, Natalie would cover for her and was always there no matter what.

So one strained conversation and a few minutes later Jalisa hung up and nodded. It was set, now all we had to do was wait for Natalie to come pick us up. Silently we got out to wait by the car, standing in the single beam of light from overhead.

"Tonight was too much fun," Chili said, bringing a smile to our faces all over again.

"Yeah, Gayle was incredible."

"She was hot and her dancers were perfect. I wish we could do some of her steps in our recital next time, that would be hot," I said, and we nodded, all agreeing.

"Yo, Kenisha, I didn't know your cousin was in that dance group. She was tight and she even knows Gayle Harmon and Tyrece. Check, you gotta get me in there."

I shrugged. I didn't know she was in it, either, but me and my cousin aren't exactly what you would call tight anymore. She lived with my grandmother in D.C. not too far from Freeman Dance Studio, but we didn't keep in touch much. Years ago we were really tight, almost like sisters. I guess we just grew apart. "I'll think about it," I said, acting like I got it like that.

"Okay, what's up with you?" Jalisa asked me.

"Me, nothing, why?" I said.

"Don't even try it," Chili said, joining in with her two cents, "you been acting all tense for a week now. You didn't even want to go to the mall yesterday. We had to drag your ass out the house."

"That's right, plus you've been in a mood all night, so what's going on?" Jalisa added.

"Nothing's going on," I said, "I told you I'm fine."

"I bet it's LaVon," Chili said to Jalisa, who nodded, agreeing with her. "You know she was in the bathroom with your girl 'bout to light it up."

"My girl who?" Jalisa asked.

"Diamond."

"Kenisha, I told you Diamond is all right. She's not trying to hook up with LaVon. I asked her. She said that they was just talking when we came in, that's all."

"Oh, please," Chili said to Jalisa, "and you believe her, Diamond would say anything. She's such a skank."

"Ow, that is harsh," Jalisa said.

"It's true."

"So why would she lie to me?" Jalisa asked.

"Why wouldn't she?" Chili said.

"This has nothing to do with LaVon or Diamond," I finally said after being left out of the conversation whose subject just happened to be me. "I told you I'm just tired, that's all."

They both looked at me, knowing better. But I just couldn't tell them that my mom and dad were fighting again.

"All right, fine, don't talk."

We got quiet for a while and I started feeling bad. Jalisa and Chili were my friends and I know I can tell them anything, so I decided to just do it. "My mom and dad are fighting again. I think they might get a divorce."

They looked at me.

As far as they know, my life is perfect.

"Well, just because they argue, doesn't mean that they're gonna get a divorce. Lots of couples argue."

"Not all the time," I said.

"Maybe," Jalisa said.

"My moms and pops don't even care enough to argue. They just stay out of the house and away from each other, away from me," Chili said sadly.

We got quiet again as we each started thinking.

Then a few minutes later, Chili opened the driver's door, switched on the satellite radio and blasted music through the empty parking lot. We started dancing and laughed and danced some more, having our own party right there in the Metro parking lot. A few cars drove by, but we were partying too hard to even notice or care.

Then reality set in as we saw two headlights turn into the parking lot. Jalisa's sister was coming and we knew we were going to hear it. She drove over, stopped her car and rolled down the window. "What are you girls doing out this late? Jalisa, I know you know better, Mom would have a fit if she knew you were hanging out this late," Natalie said.

Natalie was Jalisa's older sister by fourteen years. At twenty-nine, Natalie had been married for three years and had two-year-old twin girls. Unfortunately, her husband was in the marines and was stationed overseas. She had moved back into the family home with her two kids, so now Jalisa, with her sister and mother, had two moms on her back. Their father was also a marine on active duty overseas. So as soon as we got into Natalie's car, closed the doors and buckled our seat belts she started in with the lecture.

"Girl, what is wrong with you, calling me, knowing that I'm at work tonight. I can't just be taking off and coming out to get you. You lucky my supervisor's out this week."

"We missed the train, then Chili's car wouldn't start," Jalisa said in our defense.

Natalie shook her head as she pulled out of the deserted parking lot. "Do you have any idea what time it is? It's one-thirty in the morning," she asked and answered before Jalisa could open her mouth. "You know Mom's gonna kill you for being out this late and hanging out in D.C., too."

"We missed the train," Jalisa repeated.

"It's too dangerous out here. Anything can happen. And look at the three of you dancing in the parking lot, not a care in the world. Well, at least you had enough sense to call for a ride and not try and get a cab or something."

Chili and I looked at each other, knowing that it was best to just keep quiet.

"The video taping went longer than we thought," Jalisa said, not mentioning the after-party at the pizza place.

"Don't hand me that. There's no dance studio that's gonna to stay open this late for no recital."

"It wasn't a recital. They were shooting a video, a Tyrece Grant video, and they kept doing it over and over again to get it right. We were watching, and maybe we were in the video."

"Did you get paid?" she asked.

"No," Jalisa said.

"Well, then you weren't in the video."

I looked at Jalisa. I could only see her profile since I was in the backseat and she was sitting up front beside her sister, but I could tell that she was upset.

"You girls know you have no business coming home this late at night," she added, looking into the rearview mirror for our benefit. The lecture lasted the entire way to Chili's house. We pulled up in the driveway and Chili eagerly jumped out.

"Bye, Natalie, bye, y'all," Chili said, then hurried up the steps into the house.

Seconds later, I felt the car jerk as Natalie shifted gears and pulled off, headed to my house. She looked into the rearview mirror again, seeing me. I looked away quickly. "Kenisha, you know your mom is gonna have a fit with you coming in this late at night."

"I know," I said, speaking for the first time.

"How is she, your mom?"

"She okay."

"I haven't seen her at the gym in weeks, and how's your dad, is he still working in D.C.?"

"Yeah."

"I gotta catch up with him, my computer is acting crazy again."

"Okay," I said, half listening, trying to think of something to say just in case my mom was still awake when I got in and she wanted to give me the third degree.

"Tell your mom I said hello and that I'm gonna call her, okay. It's a shame, we all live in the same neighborhood but never see each other. Maybe I'll throw one of those back-to-school parties Mom used to throw years ago, y'all remember them?" she said, looking over to Jalisa.

Jalisa nodded, looking at her sister. "They were fun," she said, turning around to me. "Remember them?"

"Yeah, they were fun." I nodded and smiled.

"I remember Mom and I cooked a ton of hot dogs and hamburgers on the grill and everybody brought a covered dish. Man," Natalie said, chuckling to herself. "We had so much food it was insane. But it disappeared so damn fast, it was like we didn't have a thing. I remember one year Mom even had to send me out to get more food. I still can't believe Brian and his friends could eat like that. They were like vacuum cleaners."

As Natalie continued talking about the food, I could see that Jalisa's face had darkened. She went quiet. She was hurting. She always did when somebody mentioned her brother. Brian was her older brother by four years, but he was out of the picture now. At one time me and Diamond had a serious crush on him. He was so cute, but then he started doing drugs and everything changed, he changed.

It hurt Jalisa when he left, it still does. I hate seeing her like that. So I started laughing.

Natalie looked up at me in the mirror and Jalisa turned around. "Remember when Diamond fell in the pool?" I said. Jalisa's face instantly changed.

"Oh, man, yeah, man, I forgot all about that. She just got her hair done and she was showing off for that guy, what was his name?"

"Um, Scott, I think, Scott Roberts."

"That's right, she had such a crush on him."

"He was cute," I said.

"Yeah, he was," Jalisa agreed.

"I wonder whatever happened to him," I said.

"They were military and he moved when his father got transferred."

"Diamond falling in a pool, when did all that happen?" Natalie asked. "And what pool, we never had a pool in the yard."

"Yeah, we did, you remember, you, me and Brian blew up all those kiddie pools and filled them with sodas and ice, then put them all over the yard, remember?"

"Which time was this?"

"It was when we were going into seventh grade," I said. "No, eighth grade."

"That was so funny." Jalisa and I laughed again, then started telling more stories from past back-to-school parties.

"Oh, yeah, before I forget, Diamond called right after you left. Did you catch up with her?" Natalie said.

"Yeah," Jalisa said quickly.

"How come y'all three don't hang out anymore, what happened, y'all stop speaking or something?" Neither Jalisa nor I spoke. "Y'all three used to be thick as thieves when the three of you went to the dance studio together."

"She still around," Jalisa said. "We saw her tonight. Since she stays with her grandmother in D.C. most of the time in the summer, she goes to the dance studio at different times than we do, that's all."

I didn't say anything.

So a few minutes later, we pulled up in front of my house. Natalie stopped the car and I got out. "Thanks, Natalie. We really appreciate the ride. See ya, Jalisa."

"I'll call you before I go to work," she said.

"Okay, bye, and thanks again."

"Kenisha, don't forget to tell your mom hi for me."

"I will. Good night," I said, then went inside.

The foyer light had been left on as usual when I was out of the house late. It was quiet except for the low beeping of the alarm system. I went to the panel, reset it, then tipped upstairs to my bedroom. I glanced over to the master bedroom suite, the light was still on. I figured that Mom had already fallen asleep since she hadn't called my cell in over an hour, so I just went to my bedroom and went to sleep.

CHAPTER 5

Kenisha and Jalisa and Diamond

"They lit the fuse a long time ago, so I guess it was only a matter of time before there would be an explosion. Is it my fault that I am what they made me?"

—*myspace.com*

slipping in and out of the house was getting easier and easier. Mom was asleep when I got home last night and still asleep when I left this morning. I hated those tiny white sleeping pills she took, but sometimes they came in handy. I once saw this TV show that said that people who habitually take sleeping pills were trying to hide from something. I wondered what my mom was hiding from.

So as usual I hung out around the pool in our backyard in the morning, talking three-way to my girls on the phone. I had already done my laps, so I was just chilling while the hot sun warmed and dried me. Jalisa was getting ready to go to work, and Chili was still in bed.

"Did your mom say anything last night?" Chili asked.

"No, she was asleep when I got in."

"Lucky you, I heard it first thing this morning. Nat didn't have to tell my mom, she already knew. I'm grounded."

"Oooh, bummer," Chili said.

"That's a shame," I said, feeling lucky that I didn't have Jalisa's mom. She was nice and all, but she was super strict on Jalisa because she was the youngest. "Are you going to be able to go to dance class later?"

"I don't know. I hope so, I'll have to see."

"What time do you have to be at work?" Chili asked through a stifled yawn.

"Early, nine-thirty, as a matter of fact, I gotta go now."

That's another thing; Jalisa's mom insisted that she have a job in the summer. I don't think it was because they needed the money, but more like she didn't want Jalisa just hanging around doing nothing, like me and Chili.

"See y'all later."

She clicked off and Chili and I continued talking about the night before. Later at the mall I caught up with LaVon and Chili and a few other friends. I picked up a hoodie and a pair of jeans when Chili and I went shopping. LaVon and the others hung out in the food court, then I went over to his house. We watched a bootleg DVD he'd just gotten of a film still in the theaters, but we missed the end 'cause he had to go to basketball practice. So he dropped me off at home before going.

We were in the car out front kissing and saying goodbye, but then as usual he started getting all up on himself. So I pulled back. "I gotta go, my mom's probably home," I said, "and she's on my case now especially since I did that body piercing and it got infected."

"Come on, Kenisha, this junior high shit isn't working for me. You need to step up and act like you want to be with me. I'm tired of this kid stuff."

"Oh, you giving me an ultimatum or something?"

"That's right," he said.

"What about your basketball practice today?"

"What about it?"

"So when you have something to do it's okay but when I have something to do like my dance class and I have to go then it's kid stuff."

"You know that dance shit ain't as important as my basketball. That's my future."

"And dance isn't mine?" I questioned.

"You know what I mean. Every time we start hooking up, you say you got to go. All I'm saying is that you need to step up. So what's it gonna be, dance or me?"

"Another ultimatum?"

"Yeah, that's right."

I leaned over and kissed him sweet. His mouth opened and I was all inside, loving the way he made me feel, like I was loved and wanted. So we kept going, then I backed off again when I heard my name called. "Kenisha." I turned around and saw my mom standing in the open door.

"You need to leave, son, now," she said to LaVon.

He smiled and nodded. "See ya, shorty."

I got out the car and watched him drive off and prepared for new drama. As soon as the door closed behind us, my mom started in on me. "Kenisha, what is wrong with you, what was all that?"

"All what, nothing."

"Nothing, are you kidding me, are you having sex?"

"No," I said firmly, truthfully.

"Don't lie to me."

"I'm not, we're not having sex."

"I don't ever want to see that boy around here again."

"Why are you always hating on him like that?"

"Do you see yourself, you were damn near in that man's lap sitting out there."

"He's my boyfriend, he loves me."

"Kenisha, he loves what you can do for him."

"See, you're always thinking it's about sex. We have a future together, we're gonna get married and have a family and live in a house twice this size with more money than you can imagine."

"How, with what?"

"The NBA," I said, knowing that it would shut her up.

"Baby, please, I'm trying to be understanding and I know that teenage years are confusing and difficult and you have a lot of things coming at you, but…"

Okay, this was the point where I usually tuned out. I looked her straight in the eye and wondered what she had been like at fifteen. Probably alone, no friends, no boyfriend, just her and those stupid sleeping pills.

"…Do you hear me?" she said.

I didn't, but I answered anyway. "Yes, but I don't know why you don't like LaVon. He's gonna be a huge NBA basketball player and have tons of cash rolling in and…"

"Is that what you want, just to be with someone because of what they can do for you and how much money they have? What about what you can do for yourself?" She stopped, then slowed down and took my hands as we sat down on the sofa. "Kenisha, I love you more than my life and I don't want you making the same mistakes I did. Life isn't all about money and comfort. You need to understand and learn that now."

"But you did it. You have money, you married Dad and we have money, so what's so wrong with that?"

"But at what cost?"

"What?"

"Baby, some choices in life can't be changed. Your grandmother married Grandpop because he was a preacher and a man on the rise, and I married your father for basically the same reason. You and Jade have other choices for your lives, and know this, the choices you make now will follow you a long time."

"I'm going to college, if that's what you're talking about, you know that."

"Good, do that. But focus on what you want and not what your friends want or what a boyfriend wants. It's your life, you control it, nobody else. Don't just follow the crowd. You decide what's best for you, knowing that whatever you decide, you have to be able to live with the consequences."

I had no idea what all that was about, so I just nodded. "Are you going out now?" I asked her.

"Yes, I have to pick up a few things, then make a few more stops. I'll be back late, so grab something to eat."

"Okay," I said, knowing exactly what I was going to do, "I think I'll go to a movie or something, then hang out with Jalisa."

"Okay, just be careful."

She drove off and I snuck out ten minutes later and went to Freeman Dance Studio. I hadn't actually been in class in a while, so it felt great to be back. My usual class was in an hour, but since I didn't feel like being home anymore, I left early and just sat down in the back of the advanced class before ours and watched as they finished up. Jade, my cousin, was teaching this class, and Diamond, my ex-best friend, was in it.

Although our advanced class danced hip-hop and was good, this class was seriously hot. Every step and every movement was perfectly in sync. They looked like a fluid machine as they moved. I was shocked at how good they were. They mixed jazz, hip-hop and street and came out with these serious movements that were on fire.

I was checking them out so hard that I didn't even notice that Jalisa was there until she sat down right next to me.

"Hey, I didn't think you'd make it. So what are you doing here, aren't you still grounded?" she asked me.

"Yeah, but my mom was going out, so I decided to go out, too. What she doesn't know...but remember also, my punishment was for me not to take dance classes for a month. She didn't say anything about me not sitting and watching them."

We cracked up laughing, then stopped when we got shushed. Then we continued watching the dancers. "I like this song," I said, popping my shoulders to the hot hip-hop/reggae beat.

"She looks really good out there," Jalisa said about Diamond's dancing.

Her moves were tight and crisp and although I'd never admit it to her or Jalisa, she looked like a professional dancer. "She a'ight, I guess," I said.

"Don't even front, you know she's better than both of us put together."

"I beg your pardon, my stuff is hot," I said, taking mock offense, but of course everybody knew that Diamond was one of the best dancers in the school. And when we did competition, she really kicked it out.

"I'm the future businesswoman entrepreneur, you're the computer genius whiz kid and Diamond is the dancer-actress-singer. We all have our specialties."

"What about Chili?" I asked.

We looked at each other and just burst out laughing until we got shushed again. We joked again as we kept watching. "What I don't get is why you're still so tight with Diamond."

"'Cause she's our friend," Jalisa said softly.

"Your friend," I insisted.

"Whatever."

We sat awhile in silence just looking at the dancers and listening to the beat of the music. I started thinking about all those times when it was just me, Jalisa and Diamond, always together. When you saw one, the other two were close by. That's how it had been since we were four years old. We all went to the same school, had the same classes and hung out in the same dance studio. Then we just didn't anymore.

Our class started, and Jalisa participated and I watched, as per my punishment. An hour and a half later, Jalisa and I were on the Metro headed back home. "Why don't you come over and hang out for a while?"

I guess she could see that I didn't want to go home yet. "What's for dinner?"

"I don't know. I think my mom was going to grill some fish on the deck."

I smiled. Jalisa's mom had to be the best cook in the neighborhood. So there was no question about it, I was going home with her.

So we ate and hung out till way after dark, then Jalisa's mom let her drive me home even though she only had her learner's permit. But since we live in the next block, it was okay. So we pulled up into my driveway and the headlights flashed on my dad's car parked there.

"Your dad's here," Jalisa said.

I took a deep breath and let it out slowly. "Yeah."

I got out.

"Call me later," Jalisa said.

I nodded, "See ya." I waved and as soon as she pulled out, the front door opened and of course I knew it was my mom again, just like this morning with LaVon.

I turned around and saw my dad coming out with his briefcase. Relief washed over me. It was good to see him again, it seemed like forever. "Dad, you're back." We hugged.

"Hi, baby girl, how are you?" he asked, putting his briefcase on the brick step in front.

"Fine."

"Are you getting ready for school?"

"Hardly, I still got a month but I'm gonna need money to buy some new clothes."

"Remind me later, okay, baby?" he said.

"So, you hanging around or what?"

"No, baby, I gotta go," he said, then glanced up at the house and picked up his briefcase.

"Where you going?" I asked him as he headed down the steps toward his car. I followed.

"I have some things to take care of," he added as he got in the car. When the inside light came on I saw that he had three suitcases and a box in the backseat.

"You and mom argue again?"

"Talk to your mother, I gotta go, baby."

"Wait."

"Kenisha, look, I love you, you know that, but things are gonna be different around here pretty soon. You're still my daughter and that will never change."

"You're getting a divorce," I said, the words sounding like they were foreign.

"No, baby, we're not getting a divorce, that can't happen."

"Really?" I questioned.

"I swear, trust me, we're not divorcing," he said. I knew I should have felt better, relieved, but something in his voice didn't quite do it for me. There was still something going on that he wasn't telling me. "Now go talk to your mother."

"Why don't you just tell me?"

"Go, Kenisha."

"Is she awake?"

"Yeah, go, talk to your mother." He leaned down and kissed my hand. "Be good, see you soon."

"Promise," I said, but he gunned the engine and pulled away before answering.

CHAPTER 6

Hell of a Surprise

"The boredom of stagnation was endless as I sat waiting for something to happen, my life to change, my world to erupt. It did."

—*myspace.com*

SO I walked into the house and looked around as an impending sense of doom hung in the air. Something was wrong, I could feel it. It was quiet, too quiet, so I knew something was up. The foyer light was off, along with all the other lights in the house, including the upstairs hall light. I locked the door and went upstairs. When I got halfway up I heard my mom talking on the phone. Her bedroom door was open but pulled to, so I couldn't exactly make out what she was saying.

I continued upstairs and headed to my room as quietly as I could. I was an hour late for my curfew and the last thing I needed was to deal with my mom tonight. I opened my bedroom door and was just about to step inside when I heard my mom crying. I stopped.

My mom didn't cry. She yelled, she screamed, she threatened and she slapped, but she never cried, at least I never heard her. She always said that crying was for the weak. I walked down the hall and stood at her half-open door and listened.

"Mom, I don't want to deal with that now," she was saying, "and you saying I told you so isn't helping me, either. Can we or can't we?"

She went silent, so I leaned in closer, putting my ear to the open space. I assumed she was listening. "Thanks," she finally said, then listened again. "Thank you," she repeated, then sighed heavily and continued listening.

After she didn't say anything for a while, I turned to leave. I got halfway down the hall and I heard her start talking again. "No, she doesn't know. I'll tell her when she comes in tonight." She paused. "Yes, Mom, I know it's late. But she's my daughter. Okay, bye."

I stood in the hall looking back at her door, debating whether or not to go back over and knock. I finally decided to just do it. I knocked. "Mom, I'm home." The door opened more.

"Kenisha, come on in," she called out while dabbing at her eyes with one of the many crumpled-up tissues on the bed beside her.

I opened the door all the way and stepped inside. Laced with muted shadows, darkness crossed the large room. I walked over to stand beside the bed. "Sorry I'm late, I was at Jalisa's house, her mom cooked dinner, so I already ate," I said before she could start. "We hung out and I stayed, but I knew you wouldn't mind."

"And last night?" she asked.

"We missed the train and had to wait for another one. And then Jalisa's sister had to leave work and bring us home 'cause Chili forgot to put gas in the car again."

"Sit down, I want to talk to you."

"I know what you're gonna say, I'm grounded again, fine, whatever," I said before she could, then folded my arms across my chest defiantly, expecting her to recite her usual grounded-for-life speech.

"Kenisha..."

"Is that it?" I asked.

"What?" she asked. I could tell that she was out of it. "That's not what I was going to say. Sit down, we need to talk."

I sat, seeing her face clearly for the first time. She looked horrible. No makeup, her eyes red and puffy. "Somebody died, right?" I asked.

"No, why would you say that?"

"'Cause you're crying. Is Dad sick or something?" I asked, suddenly nervous. "I saw him outside, we talked, but he said that I should talk to you."

"Your dad and I are..."

"Let me guess, you're getting a divorce, right?"

"No, not exactly, we are separating."

"You're already separated, he moved out, remember?"

"That's what we need to talk about, he's moving back in..."

"Oh, well, good, it's about time," I said finally, hearing some good news.

"...and we're moving out now," she said.

"Huh?"

Her lips continued moving and I guess I was listening, but I swear I don't remember hearing anything and I don't have a clue what happened next. But I do remember getting sick. My stomach jumped and I started gagging. It was like the next few minutes evaporated into thin air and I found myself with my face in the toilet bowl. Mom was standing over me holding my hair back and rubbing my neck and shoulders with a cool, damp facecloth.

"I'm sorry, baby, I'm so sorry, baby," she kept repeating over and over again. "I never meant any of this to hurt you."

I realized that I couldn't breathe. I was fighting for air, gulping like a fish on dry land.

"Kenisha, slow down, relax, breathe slowly. We'll be fine, I promise. Everything's going to be all right."

After about five minutes, I sat down on the floor. She closed the lid and sat beside me, still stroking my hair back in place.

"You're all right," she said soothingly as she held me close and started rocking me like a toddler.

"No, I'm not all right, everything's not all right, you said you're separating and we're moving out just like that, like no big deal, so how is everything going to be all right? Why can't we just stay here? So what if Dad wants to move back in. This house is big enough for all of us. You two don't even have to see each other."

"That's just not going to work, Kenisha."

"Why not?"

"Because it won't."

"Stop treating me like I'm five years old. I'm not a child. What's going on and why do we have to move out?"

"Sweetheart, it's for the best."

"That's not an answer."

"It's going to have to be." She stood, grabbed the bathroom trash can, then walked back into her bedroom. She started grabbing the soiled tissues on her bed and putting them in the trash can. I went and stood in the doorway, watching her. She looked like a robot. When she finished, she stopped and looked around, then threw the can across the room, smashing it against the wall.

I jumped; major violence wasn't my mother's style, either. She started breathing hard, like she was panting or something. Then she started crying again. "Mom, just tell me," I said.

She spun around fast. The anger in her eyes scared the crap out of me. "Your father is moving back in with—" she paused and swallowed hard "—his girlfriend."

"His what?" My stomach sank and my heart lurched. I know I didn't hear her right. "You're lying, he would never."

"I'm sorry," she said, shaking her head steadily.

"No, there must be some mistake, Dad would never do that to us, to me."

"I'm sorry, baby."

"He's moving some other person in here, into our house and he's moving us out?" I asked, still stunned.

"It's more complicated that that, Kenisha."

"I can't believe this, is he crazy?"

"Kenisha, he's still your father."

"Since when, if he's moving us out on the street and then his girlfriend in here, then he's not my father."

"We're not moving out on the street, we're moving in with your grandmother in D.C. this Saturday."

"D.C.?"

"Yes."

"Saturday?"

"Yes."

"With Grandmom?"

"Yes."

"But y'all don't even speak to each other anymore."

"We do now. I called her, she's expecting us."

"Uh-uh, no way, he's just gonna have to come better than this and do something else. Buy his girlfriend a condo or something. I'm not leaving my house to live in no D.C."

"We have to, we don't have a choice."

"Yes, we do."

"No, we don't, baby."

"Why not?"

She looked over to the dresser. I turned around and saw an envelope lying on top of her jewelry box. I walked over and picked it up. I unfolded the paper and read the letter. "What is this?" I asked her, but she wasn't even looking at me anymore. The words were simple, but I had a hard time reading them anyway. "A temporary restraining order, he took out a restraining order against you?"

"He wants us out of the house by the end of the week, Saturday. I already made arrangements to have a…"

By this time my head was all over the place. "What? No. We're not leaving, that's not happening. This is our house, too. There must be some mistake. I was born here. My life is here. What am I supposed to do?"

"We have to, we don't have a choice. My attorney said that we need to…"

"What? Wait a minute, you have an attorney already. When did all this happen?" I asked.

I looked at the restraining order again and saw the date on top, then put it back on the dresser. Without saying another word, I walked out. By the time I got to my bedroom, the tears were pouring down my face. My life had changed just that quickly; my life was over as far as I was concerned.

In my bedroom, as soon as I turned my lights on, the television went on, too, it was automatic, but the sound was always on mute. I sat on the side of my bed and stared at the screen. Some video was on, but I wasn't paying attention. I just sat there, I had no idea how long. All I knew was that my head was starting to hurt again and my stomach was still all twisted up.

So I grabbed my cell and called my dad. His voice mail picked up. I hung up and called again, but this time I punched in 911, knowing that he'd call me back as soon as he got the message. But he didn't. So I waited. Fifteen minutes later, I was still waiting. So I called him again and this time I left a message.

"So what's up, you stop talking to me, too? Yeah, I talked

to Mom and I saw the restraining order. Are we really moving or what? What's up with that? Call me back."

I couldn't believe it. So here I was, living my life like everything was cool, but really everything was all messed up, and nobody even said anything to me. So how was I supposed to wrap my head around this? I went out, then came back, and then I had to leave my house, move out and go live with my grandmother. A woman I barely saw once a year.

I heard my mom in her bedroom. I had no idea what she was doing. It sounded like she was throwing things or moving furniture or something, 'cause it was really loud. I knew I had a million questions to ask her, but I couldn't think of a single one. But then again, I didn't really want to deal with her right then anyway. All I knew was that her and my dad really messed up.

I looked over at the TV. Tyrece Grant's video came on, not the one he'd just made last night, but they were talking about it. I guess somebody from the set went back and told them about it, 'cause they even had a video clip from the front of the dance studio. It was all shaky like somebody did it with their cell phone, but it was clear enough to see what was going on.

It was Tyrece and he was walking out with a few of his boys, then there was a quick glimpse of some of the people around. I saw my cousin walking by, too. Then a few minutes later there was a scuffle, and it sounded like shots fired and everybody started ducking down and running at the same time. I saw LaVon for a brief second.

I reached for my remote to turn the volume up, but the

scene stopped and went back to talking about Tyrece's career. I muted the sound again and called LaVon. He didn't answer, so I left a message, then hung up and tossed the phone on the bed beside me. As soon as I did, the phone vibrated. I answered, my voice still trembling. "Hello," I said, thinking it was about time my dad called me back.

Wrong.

"Damn, girl, you sound like shit, your mom must have grounded your ass for life," Chili said, and Jalisa giggled via our usual three-way conversation. "See, I told you she couldn't sneak in again without getting caught."

"What'd you get," Jalisa asked, "another two weeks?"

"I can't talk right now," I said. My head was pounding. All I could think about was waking up from this nightmare.

"Oh, snap, first no dance class for a month and now your mom is taking your cell phone, too. That's just cruel," Jalisa said, assuming.

"Nah, I'm just tired. I still have my cell."

Jalisa and Chili started talking about what was going on, but I didn't say anything for a while. Their drama was the least of my worries right then. Besides, I wasn't sure what to say. Yeah, Jalisa and Chili were my girls and yeah, we usually told each other everything, but this was different. This was personal, this was my family.

So right now while they were talking about the video I was debating, going back and forth about whether or not I should say anything. But come Saturday they were gonna find out anyway when some big old truck pulled up and loaded all my stuff, so I guessed I'd better tell them before they found out some other way.

Then I'm thinking, maybe it won't happen after all. Maybe it's just one of those things and it'll all blow over in a day or two. Maybe Dad will come back and everything will be just like it was before. But I know better. Denial. I knew that this had been coming for a long time. So that's it, without thinking, I blurted it out. "My mom is leaving my dad."

It went silent for a minute. I wasn't sure if they even heard me, so I said it again. "My mom is leaving my dad."

Jalisa was the first to say something. "Aw, girl, I sorry. Are you okay?"

"Damn, that's too bad," Chili added. "I wonder if there's any video of me when I was talking to one of Tyrece's dancers."

"Where she going?" Jalisa asked, ignoring Chili.

"To D.C. to live with my grandmother," I answered.

"Are you okay?" Jalisa said again.

"Yeah, I'm fine," I said.

"You can visit her, right?" Chili said encouragingly.

"She wants me to move, too," I said slowly, hearing the words leave my mouth for the first time. They tasted bitter, almost angry. The line went silent again at all three ends. None of us knew what to say next.

"Why, you can just live with your pops, can't you?" Chili said.

"She has to go where her mom tells her," Jalisa said.

"No, she don't. She can live with her dad."

"You don't get it," Jalisa said.

"I do so. She can just stay with her pops."

"No, I can't. I have to go, too," I finally said, interrupting their argument.

"But why?" Chili insisted.

"I don't know, that's just how it is, okay?" I snapped. I wasn't in the mood to debate and discuss the issue anymore. I was simply stating fact and ending it there.

"You don't have to bite my head off, I just asked," Chili said.

"I know, I'm sorry, it's just that this is so wrong. Their drama is so messed up, now I gotta deal with it."

"I know, girl. But maybe they'll get back together. I mean, married people separate all the time and then get back together, right?" Jalisa said.

"I don't know, maybe, I know that I need to catch up with my dad and seriously talk to him about this," I said.

"Okay, so maybe it'll only be for a short time," Chili insisted. "After a few days you'll be right back here where you belong."

"Yeah, that's right, you never know, it might happen. After a few days away your dad is gonna want you and your mom back and it'll be like nothing ever happened," Jalisa added.

I knew my friends were only trying to be supportive and all, but listening to them now only made me want to just hang up the phone and get it over with. "Yeah, maybe," I said, hoping that it would be just like that.

"So when are you leaving?"

"Soon," I said, without being more specific. I didn't want to hear a whole new drama when I told them that it might be in a few days.

"Soon, that can mean anytime," Chili said. "Soon like in after school starts or soon like when you're already in college?"

"Speaking about school, what about school, it starts next month," Jalisa said.

"Yeah, how are you going to get all the way back here every day if you live in D.C.?" Chili asked.

"Commute, probably until my dad buys me the car he promised for my birthday next month," I said.

"One thing's for sure, there's no way they gonna want you to leave Hazelhurst, your father's even on the parent advisory board, right?"

"That's right, and your mom's, like, vice president of the PTO."

"Yeah," I said, knowing that none of that mattered anymore.

Silence erupted again as we all three realized the answer at the same time: I wasn't going to attend Hazelhurst anymore.

"You can stay with me," Jalisa offered.

"Or me," Chili added.

"I don't know what's gonna happen about that yet."

"Did you tell LaVon?" Chili asked.

"No, not yet." Truth was, all this was happening so fast, I'd forgotten all about LaVon. "I gotta go, I'll talk to y'all later."

I didn't want to hear them saying goodbye, so I just closed my cell quickly and lay down on my bed. I curled up with my childhood teddy bear but the soft bed and fluffy pillows did little to calm my fears. I was scared. I closed my eyes and just waited for sleep so that I could wake up from this nightmare. When I did I'll know it wasn't true.

So I dreamt that I was falling, but it wasn't into some deep, dark abyss or some bottomless pit like you always hear about in the movies, it was into bright, blinding sunlight and everything around me was moving in slow motion except me. I could see cars and house and people's faces, but I was moving really fast. My hair was being pulled back and my arms were flapping, I was trying to fly, but the harder I tried, the faster I fell. Then it hit me to just relax and let it happen, like what they say about quicksand. So I do. I let go and let it happen.

Nothing changed, I just kept falling.

CHAPTER 7

Ready... Set...

"Between here and there is nowhere and everybody wants to get out. So you scream at the top of your lungs for someone to see you. Question: what's real and what's not?"
—*myspace.com*

I WAS still falling when I woke up.

So then it was Wednesday, early, and the house phone kept ringing, but I just ignored it and stayed in bed. My mom stopped by a few times, but I pretended like I was asleep and she went away. Sometime later the doorbell rang. I got up thinking it was for me, but then I looked out my bedroom window and saw this big-ass truck parked out front and then these men were unloading a ton of boxes and bringing them inside.

It had started.

I picked up my phone and called my dad's cell, then his hotel room and then his office phone. He didn't answer any of them, so I left messages then called LaVon.

"Hey, I was just about to call you," he said, lying, of course. He said that to everybody when they called him.

"I tried calling you last night," I said.

"I was out late," he said, being vague about what he had been doing, as usual.

"I need to talk to you," I said.

"You're moving, yeah, I heard," he said, way too nonchalantly.

Okay, now I was pissed again. First of all, his whatever attitude was all wrong. Then it was more like he was bored with the news of my moving rather than upset about me leaving.

Now the first thing I thought was that word was already on the street about my mom and dad breaking up, but then it hit me that I only told Chili and Jalisa and I know my mom didn't tell anyone else. I needed to seriously talk to my girls about talking my business.

"How'd you hear?" I asked, suspecting that it was probably Jalisa since we all go way back as friends.

"So when you leaving?" he asked, not answering my question.

"Damn, LaVon, can't you at least try to put a little heart into it?" I asked.

"What you want from me, shorty, to start crying and act like a punk or something?"

"I didn't say all that, but you acting like it's no big deal, like you don't even care that I'm leaving."

"'Cause it ain't. You're only moving to D.C. That's, like, thirty-five minutes away. It's not like you're doing serious distance."

"Didn't whoever tell you that my mom and dad are breaking up?"

"Yeah, Chili told me. So what? Shit happens all the time," he said.

That snitch, now I was seriously beyond pissed off and LaVon with his dumb-ass didn't even realize that he'd just confirmed that Chili told him I was moving.

So now I'm thinking, what was her drama? I'd told her that I was gonna call LaVon, he was supposed to be my boyfriend, not hers. So why did she have to step up and tell him first?

"So what you doing today?" he finally asked.

"I gotta do some stuff, why."

"I was thinking about coming over later, a'ight?"

"Yeah, I'll be here."

"A'ight, see ya."

I closed my phone, disappointed. It used to be really nice being with LaVon, but lately he was just acting like another fool. All he cared about was basketball and getting some, and since I wasn't putting out, I knew he was getting it from someone else, I just didn't know who. Then Diamond came to mind.

So now I was thinking back, Chili once told me months ago that Diamond was checking LaVon out right after her sweet sixteen birthday party, but I didn't believe her at first.

Then everything changed and Diamond started acting all crazy strange, so we just started dissing her. Jalisa kept being friends with her, but I was tired of dealing with her drama.

Anyway, I got dressed and a few minutes later my mom came in and we had a conversation about what I wanted to pack to go where, to D.C. or to storage. She talked and I just nodded 'cause I had in my head that none of this was actually going to happen 'cause I was gonna fix this. I was gonna call my dad and make this right again.

Later I called my dad's cell phone like a million times, but he still didn't return my calls. So I called his office again and his receptionist, Mrs. Taylor, connected me with his assistant, Courtney Lawson. Courtney used to be down, but she changed.

She was like nine or ten years older than me. When she first got the job, she didn't know anything. I even had to show her some stuff. But then a few months later, she started acting all important, like she just about owned the place. And now she was a snide-talking wannabe with serious delusions of grandeur, plus she had a thing for my dad, so he kept her around to stroke his ego, among other things.

I knew he was doing her. Everybody knew.

Once, one day last year, I dropped by his office in D.C. late after dance practice and found the two of them locked up in his office, took them close to five minutes to open the door and when he did his shirt was zipped up in his pants and Courtney had big red marks on her knees. Guess why? Skank. My mom must have known he was playing around on her. I didn't know why my dad didn't just fire her ass to keep the peace.

So anyway, I asked to speak with my dad.

"I'm sorry, your father isn't available," she said all cold and businesslike.

"I know he's busy, Courtney, but I need to talk to him now. So can you go get him out of whatever meeting he's supposed to be in and tell him that his daughter is on the phone waiting," I said, daring her to say something else.

She put me on hold. I swear she came back ten minutes later. "He's still unavailable. I'll tell him you called. Is there anything else?"

"Uh, yes, there's something else, you let him know that I'm on my way down there—"

"Coming down here won't change the fact that he's un-available," she interrupted. "He has meetings planned all day, and most are out of the office."

"Okay, fine, then tell him that I'm calling the police and reporting that my father beat me, then I'm calling the news and then this fat-ass list of clients I just found on his desk in his home office."

"Blackmail is so unbecoming, and I know for a fact that there is no client list on your father's desk at home. I've been in his home office, I've seen his desk."

"Lying on your back or kneeling underneath," I quipped under my breath, but loud enough for her to hear me. She didn't reply, so I just let it lie there. "So are you sure that I don't have a client list?" I opened my laptop, typed in a few keys, then pulled up my dad's company's client list. I smiled. I saved everything.

"Positive," she said, "so why don't you go play with your little friends at the mall and let your father take care of his business, know what I mean? F-Y-I, don't bluff if you can't back it up."

"F-Y-I, there is a client list, aka James Lewis holiday card list, it includes names, addresses, phone numbers, wives' and children's names, and even likes and dislikes,"

I told her. Then started running off client names that my dad sent to my computer last year 'cause he asked me to take care of his holiday gift-giving and mailing list.

The line went silent, but I could tell she was still there, 'cause I could hear her breathing. "So tell him that I gotta go make a few phone calls, know what I mean." The skank wasn't sure if I was serious or not. .

"Hold on," she said finally.

I hung up. I was tired of this game.

My dad called back two minutes later. I didn't pick up, I decided that I was unavailable.

Jalisa called and wanted to stop by, but I told her that I was on my way to D.C. I lied. I didn't want to be bothered. Before I got dressed I called LaVon again, but he didn't answer.

The rest of the day went downhill from there. My mom was packing and I could hear her talking on the phone to my grandmother again. They were arguing as usual.

I went to bed early.

I slept mostly, half expecting to be falling again.

I did.

CHAPTER 8 ..

...Go

"Finding yourself where you don't want to be is like sitting in hell waiting for a cool breeze to come along. You fight and struggle against status quo, just give it up, relief ain't coming."
—*myspace.com*

Thursday was over fast, I don't even remember it. So then it was Friday. I opened my eyes to wait for my life to get back to where it was. I still said that this has to be a dream. But reality was taking its sweet-ass time to get back around to me. I just lay there thinking.

My mom had been packing her stuff like crazy since last night and all day yesterday and the day before that.

It had been two days and I still wasn't in the mood to do anything. I just hung around all day in my room dealing or rather not dealing, interrupted occasionally by my mom stopping by to check on me and my cell phone going unanswered. The last time, she knocked on my bedroom door, then came in and sat on the bed beside me.

"Kenisha, this is going to be okay, I promise you." I just looked at her. She had to kidding. "If you want to talk, I'm here."

"There's nothing to talk about, right? We're out of here. It's over, the house, the cars, the clothes, the money."

"Nothing's over, we still have everything we need. Having money isn't having worth. It'll be good, you'll see. Your grandmother is really looking forward to seeing you and spending some time with you and Jade's excited, too. Nothing will really change, you'll see."

"Nothing will really change?" I asked, looking at her like she was nuts. "You mean nothing like my address, my school, my friends, my family, that nothing?"

"Kenisha, be positive. You still have your family and friends, and the new school won't be that bad. This will be a good thing in the long run, you'll see."

"I've been going to Hazelhurst Academy since first grade, I know the teachers, and they know me. So when it comes to college letters of recommendation, what am I supposed to do? Those new teachers won't know me, and what about all my extracurricular activities for the college applications?"

"Everything will be transferred and college will be fine. You'll get into the school you want."

"How, with what, my college fund?"

"Your father will take care of that."

"Yeah, like he's taking care of me living here?" I said, questioning her raging assumption that he was gonna actually step up and do anything. But the vindication I hoped to feel fell flat.

"You have every right to be upset and scared. I am, too. But be positive, everything will work out for the best. Why don't you give Jalisa and Diamond a call and go to the mall?"

I shook my head. Her validation didn't make me feel any better.

"Okay then, why don't you come downstairs and get something to eat. You'll feel better."

"I'm not hungry," I said.

"You've barely eaten anything in almost two days. You need to eat something. You can't starve yourself to death up here."

"I'm not hungry."

"Okay, you must have questions about all this."

"Questions, I was here, remember, I heard the arguments. It's not like I'm new to this. You and Dad have been fighting full-force since the last day of school. I guess I should have seen this coming."

"I know, sweetie, but I just need you to understand I did this for you. I'm trying to do the right thing now to make a better future for you and Jade..."

"You did what for me, and what does this have to do with Jade?" I asked. "And how can a husband put his wife and daughter out? Isn't that like against the law or impossible or something? This house is just as much yours as it is his, didn't your lawyer tell you that? And if you have a prenup, just break it. Everybody knows he's been doing Courtney for years."

"Kenisha," she said, raising her voice slightly.

"No, Mom, no, I'm not stupid and I'm not blind.

Give me some credit. Teenagers always get a bad rep, but y'all adults do stuff all the time and we're just supposed to not see it?"

"It's complicated."

"Complicated how? Step up to him and get your half."

"Kenisha, I wish so much for you and Jade...."

"Jade again, what is it with Jade? You spend most of your time with Jade."

"Jade is—" she said, then paused.

"I know, she's your niece and you were close to Aunt Hannah Mae, I get that, but what does she have to do with any of this now?"

"If I could do it over, I swear I would, but it's too late and I can't take any of this back. I messed up and I'm just so sorry."

"Mom what are you talking about, messed up what? Did you do something illegal or have an affair or something? Is that why all this is happening?"

She looked around my bedroom and saw that it was exactly the same except for the boxes and rolls of bubble wrap against the wall. "You need to start packing. The trucks are coming early." She got up and left and that was it for our talk.

She didn't say much to me the rest of the day, she just let me have my space. I guess she could see I needed it or maybe she needed it.

After that I was mainly just riding low the rest of the day. Chili and Jalisa called a few times, I talked to them once or twice, then just turned my cell off again. I wasn't in the mood to hear no sad drama about missing me. They stopped by Wednesday and Thursday, but I didn't want to be bothered, so I told them I was busy doing stuff that I wasn't. I felt bad but for real, I just didn't want to be bothered.

Oh, and LaVon's tired ass never did show up.

The next morning, Saturday, three moving vans pulled up in front of my house early, at 6:00 a.m. I was already up. I watched them from the upstairs window. Seven men got out the trucks. The driver from the first truck grabbed a clipboard and walked over and rang the doorbell. My mom answered. They talked a minute while the other six men opened the backs of the trucks and started pulling out big carpet swatches and other stuff, dumping them in the driveway like we was having some kind of weird yard sale.

There was no way I was going to be sitting there while people I didn't even know took my life apart piece by piece.

So I started packing like my life depended on it. I kept packing and packing like crazy. I heard my mom and some man talking outside my bedroom, but I just kept packing. Everything was going in the boxes—books, DVD movies, clothes, shoes, everything. Four hours later, my bedroom was looking like one of those storage bin places on the side of the road. I had my entire life stuffed inside the boxes.

"Kenisha," my mom said as she knocked on my bedroom door.

Everything was scattered all over the place. I was waist-deep in boxes, tape and wrap, sitting on the floor after I had just pulled my thousand or so CDs off the shelf. "Yeah," I called out to her.

She opened the door. "They're ready for your room."

I stared at her a minute. I swear I had no idea what she was saying. I saw her lips moving, but that was it. Then this man came to the door behind her and he looked at me and then at my room like he was sizing things up. And I knew right then, I mean, really knew for the first time that this was for real. I was leaving my house for good.

I grabbed my purse and my cell and I walked out.

The house was almost empty already. My mom obviously wasn't playing around, she was seriously taking everything. I swear it looked like she had even scraped the wallpaper off the walls, wow, she even took the lightbulbs out the sockets and the switch plates off the walls. I laughed to myself, my dad's jaw was gonna drop off when he saw that place.

I went into her bedroom. It was completely empty, curtains, carpet, doorknobs, everything. The two guest bedrooms were also empty and so were the living room and dining room. There were two guys walking around carrying boxes and two in my dad's office packing his stuff.

Then there was a guy in the kitchen and one in the family room. I decided the only place to be was out of there.

I stood in the empty foyer and called Jalisa, but before I could even say hi, she started in on me.

"Kenisha, you know I shouldn't even be speaking to your butt. So what's up? Where have you been, Chili and I tried calling you. You just like dropped off the radar. Just 'cause you might be moving don't mean you can't pick up a phone and call somebody."

"You gotta go to work this morning?" I asked, not bothering to respond to her rant.

"Nah, I don't go in until late this afternoon. I hate working the afternoon shift. You have no idea how many assholes want to sneak into a stupid movie. It only costs eight bucks, just give up the green and walk in, it's so stupid," she added, complaining about her job like she always did.

"Is your mom home?" I asked her.

"Nah, she went out shopping with Natalie. Why, what's up?"

"I gotta get out of here."

"What, you and your mom get into it again?"

"No, my mom and I are moving out. I told you, we're gonna live with my grandmother in D.C., we're moving today," I said simply, as if it were the most natural thing in the world.

"Yeah, right," she said, obviously discounting what I'd told her. "Are you going to be able to go to dance class next week? I might not."

"Jalisa, I'm serious, it's today, I'm moving today. There are three huge trucks packing our stuff up even as I speak."

She went quiet for a second. "I'll be right over."

"No, the guys are here to move my stuff and I don't want to be here. Can I come over?"

"Yeah," she said without hesitation.

I stuffed my cell back in my purse and headed out the

front door, then turned at the last second to see that my mom was coming downstairs. The man with the clipboard was right behind her. She was pointing across the room and then she glanced over and saw me standing in the doorway. "Kenisha, do you have everything marked for storage and for your grandmother's house?"

"Yeah," I said, then moved aside as two men walked past me carrying boxes. I looked at them and shook my head. "I'm going over to Jalisa's house."

"Don't be too long, I want to get to your grandmother's house by noon, and I still have a lot to do today."

I nodded numbly, then turned and left. As soon as I stepped outside, two huge gaping holes faced me. One truck was already completely filled. I didn't want to think about it anymore. So I just walked away.

When I got to Jalisa's house, I saw Natalie's car sitting in the driveway. I started to ring the bell, but the door opened too fast. Jalisa was standing on the other side of the door. The expression on her face said it all. The two of us had been together a long time. This was our first real separation.

We went inside through the kitchen then out on the deck overlooking the backyard. I leaned on the rail and stared out while Jalisa sat cross-legged on a lounge chair. We were silent for the first few minutes as I guess we tried to figure out what to say.

"I hate them. I wish they were dead," I hissed quietly.

"Kenisha, don't be saying stuff like that," Jalisa said quickly.

"I do, seriously," I said, "I swear I can't help it. They

piss me off so bad. Why couldn't he just keep it in his pants and why couldn't she just deal with it or at least divorce him and keep the house? Why do we have to move? They're only thinking about themselves. They don't care about me or what I want."

"I thought they might wait until you were in college or something. You know, what's another year?"

"That's what I'm saying."

"So are you still going to Hazelhurst?"

"I don't know," I said, "I doubt it."

"That's messed up."

"I know, I'm seriously screwed, all my college courses, my extracurricular activities, and even my recommendations. I won't know any of those new teachers. How are they gonna recommend me?"

"It'll work out," Jalisa promised.

"How? No, Jalisa, it won't work out. This is messed up." I started to walk around, too restless to stay in one place. I grabbed my purse off the rail.

"Kenisha, where you going?"

"I gotta go, I'll see you later."

I walked over to LaVon's house, but his sister told me that he was out and wouldn't be back until late. Figures, the one time I needed him, he was unavailable.

By the time I got home, they were working on filling up the third truck. My world disappeared into the back of the truck in less then five and a half hours. Everything I knew was gone. I walked into the empty house and saw the bare walls and realized that this wasn't just a bad dream. This was a nightmare. I was being kicked out of the only house I ever knew. I went upstairs to my bedroom, it was empty. I closed the door.

I walked over and sat on the once cushioned window seat with my eyes closed as my mom's voice echoed through the empty house. I heard her calling me, but I didn't care. I wasn't in the mood to listen to it anymore. Whatever had happened between her and my dad didn't involve me.

"Kenisha," she called out again, then I heard her walking up the steps and down the hall toward my bedroom, her heels clicking on the hardwood floors like chattering teeth. She called my name a few more times before she came to the door. She knocked once, then entered.

"Kenisha," she said, poking her head in and spotting me across the empty open space. "Come on, Kenisha, we need to leave now."

"I'm not going," I said, knowing it sounded childish, but I didn't care anymore. "I'm staying."

"Come on, Kenisha, we don't have time for this."

"No," I said adamantly.

She walked over and sat down beside me. "Kenisha, I know you're upset and I know that right now you don't understand everything that's going on, but just trust me. I need to leave here and I'm not leaving you by yourself."

"I won't be by myself. Dad will be here in a few. I'll stay with him."

She looked hurt, then reached up and wiped the tear on my cheek. "Honey, we gotta go."

"No, you go, I'm staying," I said stubbornly.

"You can't stay, Kenisha."

"Why not? This is my house, too. Why can't I stay?"

She sighed heavily. I could hear the twisted knot in her throat as she gurgled, then started crying. "I'm sorry, baby, I'm sorry, I'm so sorry, I messed up bad. But I thought... I'm so sorry."

"What, what is it?" I asked as I wrapped my arm around her shoulders. She broke down completely. We sat there in each other's arms, crying until we were cried dry.

Later she stood and walked to the open door. "We have to go now, your dad will be here soon."

Suddenly I didn't want to see this house anymore. We went downstairs, walked outside, got in her car and drove off. We led, the trucks followed. That was that.

CHAPTER 9

A New Home

"Why is it that it always seems to take longer to get where you really want to be and shorter to be where you really don't want to get? Life seems like an eternity sometimes then other times it goes by in a flash."

—*myspace.com*

I plugged my earbuds in, turned away and stared out the window and saw the last of my world dissolve in a blur behind me. I felt queasy, sick to my stomach and my head was spinning like a merry-go-round. Everything I knew was now gone and there was nothing I could do about it. For the first time in my life I hated my father.

"Kenisha..." my mom said. When I didn't answer, she looked over, then tugged at the cord around my neck, pulling an earpod out. "Kenisha."

"I don't want to talk about it," I said before she could start talking about this new life she had planned for me.

"We need to talk."

"Why, is something gonna change? If we do talk, will they put everything back in our house? Will Dad change his mind?"

"No."

"So why talk?"

"It might help you feel better."

"I doubt it."

"Kenisha, bottom line is we need to stick together. We can't alienate each other." I didn't respond. "You act like we're moving to the other side of the universe. The Metro goes right into Virginia, and your grandmother lives just a few blocks away. You'll still see your girlfriends."

"What about LaVon?"

"LaVon isn't the only boy in the world. There are plenty of guys in D.C. As a matter of fact, your grandmother's next-door neighbor, Terrence Butler, is a very nice young man. He's going into his freshman year at Howard, majoring in engineering. He's very smart. He graduated high school early and even attended…"

"Are you doing his PR now, Mom?"

"What?"

"You're going on and on about some guy like he's some kind of saint. He's probably just another wannabe drugged-up gangster hoodrat."

"A what?"

"A hoodrat, you know, someone who lives in the hood."

"Not everybody who lives in D.C. is a wannabe drugged-up gangster hoodrat. I don't know where you get that."

"The news, they be killing each other all over the place.

Every time you turn it on, somebody shot somebody else. I'd be surprised if there was anybody left in Chocolate City."

"Don't believe everything you read in the newspaper or hear on television. The media has a tendency to seek out the worst in our people. There are some very nice people in D.C. Just like there are wannabe drugged-out gangster hoodrats in the pricey exclusive suburbs of Virginia and Maryland and Boston and London and every place else. Where a person comes from isn't who that person is, you should know that by now."

"But every night somebody has shot up some nightclub or did a drive-by. D.C. is nothing but hood city and anybody who's from there is just a hoodrat."

"Including me?" she asked.

"No, I didn't say that. I mean, there are exceptions, like you and grandmom."

"Oh, thanks, I'm an exception now."

"Yeah, you know what I mean," I said.

"And Jade, is she an exception, too?"

"Jade, I don't know yet, the jury's still out on her."

"Uh-huh, okay, we'll see," she said in that haughty I-know-best voice she always used whenever she thought she knew something I didn't. "Just do me a favor. Don't judge everything and everyone by what you think you know. My mother always said that appearances matter, and I'm not so sure that's true. You'd be surprised," she said, more to herself than to me. "It's the beautiful people that have the wickedest lies."

I didn't answer. I was thinking about my dad, beautiful people and wicked lies. He had everything, a wife and daughter, a business, a great house and on paper he looked like a saint, but here I was moving out anyway. Mom was right, so much for appearances.

So I've been thinking about my family all morning.

Don't get me wrong, I love my family, my grandmother and my cousin and all, but the thing is, I really don't know them. I mean, I know them, but I really don't know them. I have all these half-faded memories of when I was a kid and all, but that's it.

My mom stopped taking me over there to visit years ago. Then on my birthday a few years back, I think her and my grandmother must have had some kind of argument, 'cause they stopped talking for a while, but that's all I know.

But before that, I remember that she would always go and get my cousin, Jade, and she would come over to the house and we'd spend all afternoon together shopping at the mall or hanging out at the movies or at the park. Then my mom would take her back home and we'd do the same thing all over again the next day. Then it stopped, no reason, it just stopped.

Now I run into Jade sometimes at the dance studio. We used to chat a little bit at first, but both of us knew we had nothing much in common, so we just basically said hi or nodded and let it go at that.

My cousin Jade was three years older than me and went to Howard University in the city. She was on campus, I think, but she still lived with our grandmother sometimes, but nobody ever talked about her mother. I didn't know why. She had been my mom's other sister,

Hannah Mae, the oldest, who died of a drug overdose. But as I said, nobody ever talked about her mother.

So forty-five minutes later, we pulled up in Old City D.C. in front of a three-story, stone facade building with dark green shutters. The house looked small and cramped and I wondered how all of us were gonna fit in there. But at least it had grass, even if it was only on three sides. The fourth side was attached to the house next door. It definitely wasn't what I remembered.

Spewed with dramatically colored rosebushes, the rest of the lawn was being cut by a guy wearing an untucked white T-shirt, jeans, sneaks and wired earbuds plugged in both ears. He looked up as we drove up, then turned and went back to work on the side.

The house was on the corner, and we parked right in front. Then one of the trucks pulled up behind us. The other two had turned off a while ago, just before we left Virginia. I got out of the car, stumbled and almost tripped 'cause I was looking up at the house. It seemed a whole lot smaller than I remembered, but even still, it was almost twice as big as the other houses on the block.

So I walked up to the front door. It was closed and the curtains were drawn tight. It looked like nobody was even home. So I turned to check out what my mom was doing, then I heard the front door open. I turned around again.

A gray-haired woman, petite, the same size as my mom, walked out on the open front porch. She looked me up and down. "So aren't you going to say hello and give your grandmother a hug?" she said, half smiling, like cracking her face made it hurt.

"Hi, Grandmom," I said mechanically.

We hugged awkwardly, then she held on to my hand and really checked me out. "Girl, you're the spitting image of your mother but tall just like your daddy."

"Thanks," I said, not sure if I was supposed to consider that a compliment or not. Somehow I doubted it.

"Where's your mom?" she asked, still staring at me.

"Hi, Momma, it's been a long time. You look good," my mom said, forcing a smile as she walked up onto the porch. We both turned to see my mom carrying a box.

"You're late, you said you'd be here an hour ago."

"It took longer than I expected. The movers are ready to get started."

"All right, then, let's get this done. You take your old bedroom and Kenisha can have the third floor with Jade."

"Is Jade here?" my mom asked.

"No, she went out a few minutes ago. She'll be back later."

"Kenisha, do me a favor and take this upstairs," my mom said, then handed me the box she was carrying. "After that you can go check out your bedroom. It's the third floor back."

"A'ight. Where you want this at?"

"What was that?" my grandmother asked me as I grabbed the box from my mother.

I looked at her, figuring she must be losing her hearing or something. "I said a'ight," I repeated, louder.

"I'm not deaf, Kenisha. I am, however, surprised by your atrocious grammar. Your guttural vernacular is bad enough, but your syntax is intolerable. You see, around here we speak proper English, none of that slang Ebonics stuff. Do you understand me?"

I nodded.

"Do you understand me?" she repeated more crisply.

"Yes, I understand you," I said coolly.

"And watch your attitude, young lady. In this house everyone and everything matters."

"Yes," I said. I took the box and just as I did, I saw the guy who was mowing the lawn walking up. I knew he must have heard what my grandmother had just said. Pity, 'cause he was cute, too.

So I went inside pissed. As soon as the door closed behind me, I heard my grandmother talking to my mom about my manners, or as she said, my lack thereof. My mom was just nodding and saying nothing to defend me. At thirty-four she was acting like she was ten years old again.

So once inside, I looked around quickly and the first thing I noticed was that the place smelled old and musty, like it had been shut up for years. I walked into the front living room and took a look around. It was bigger than I thought and it had these seriously old pictures of all these people on the walls. Portraits, none of them smiling.

I kept looking around, realizing that I didn't remember any of it. The sofa and chairs all had plastic wrapped on them and so did the lamps and throw pillows. I chuckled to myself 'cause it looked so stupid. What was she expecting, a thunderstorm inside?

I peeked into the dining room. It was big and like the living room it had really high ceilings.

I went back to the foyer, then over to the stairs. Up two

floors I peeked into the first bedroom. I assumed it was mine 'cause it was completely empty. I sat the box on the floor and checked it out.

It was big; the floors were hardwood, not the perfect new polished kind I used to have in my old house. These floors were old and thick. They creaked when I walked and there were a few nails sticking up along the baseboard. The ceiling was high with the same detailing. I'm not saying it was nice, but it could have been worse.

There were these big bay windows on one end and a serious built-in armoire with mirrored doors on the other. I went over to the window and looked out. On the third floor in a neighborhood surrounded by two-story houses, I could almost see ten blocks away, but it was mainly treetops and telephone lines.

I went over and checked out the armoire. It was nice but small. So I looked around for more closet space 'cause there was no way all my clothes were gonna fit in there. There was another door so I went over, opened it and looked inside. It was a walk-in closet, but it already had clothes on one half. I started checking out some of the wardrobe, figuring that it was Jade's. She had some decent stuff, considering.

So off that room there was another door. I looked inside and saw that it was the bathroom. I guess we had to share. There was another door, so I checked it out. It was Jade's room. I went in and looked around then all of a sudden I felt like a snoop, so I went back to my room and closed the doors behind me.

I heard my mom and my grandmother talking downstairs on the second floor. They were loud, almost arguing, but I couldn't really make out what they were talking about, different house, same old drama.

I went over and looked out the window again. The lawn mower guy was walking around out back. I couldn't see him clearly, so I tried to open the window, but it was stuck. I knelt closer to sit down on the window seat to try and get a better view.

"Kenisha."

I turned around and saw Jade standing in my doorway.

"Hey," she said, not particularly smiling.

I smiled anyway, I guess from relief. It had been a long time since Jade and I spoke, but she still looked the same and even after seeing her onstage dancing the other night she looked the same as I remembered before. "Hey," I said, "I saw you the other night at Freeman dancing with Gayle Harmon. I wanted to catch up with you, but I had to leave. You looked incredible up there."

"Thanks," she said coldly. "We have to share the closet and bathroom and I usually take a shower in the morning," she said. I nodded silently. "Also I cleared the bottom two drawers in the vanity and I use the first sink, you can take the other one by the window. There was a medicine cabinet on that side. I never use it, so it's already empty, so just put your stuff in there. I'll be moving back into the dorms at the end of the month, so all this is temporary." She waited a second, then turned to leave.

"Jade," I heard myself saying before I could stop, "thank you." She nodded but didn't bother turning around. I heard the wood creak as she walked down the hall and headed back downstairs. Why in the world was I thanking her? I asked myself.

I went back downstairs a few minutes later and sat out on the back stoop to avoid the mess going on inside with the movers. I sat and watched the lawn mower guy put the stuff away in the big shed out back. I was right, he was cute. He had these seriously light-colored eyes with this sweet caramel-colored skin and light brown kinky hair with blondish tips. But the thing that hit me was that he was seriously nicely built 'cause he had taken his T-shirt off and had tucked it into his back pocket. He had serious LL Cool J biceps, triceps and abs and a totally flat stomach with this sweet little tattoo on his upper arm. I couldn't really make out what it was, but it looked like a butterfly, but that didn't sound right.

So I was staring at him like I had no sense at all, trying to figure out what the tattoo was, then he turned and started watching me watch him. By this time I was totally in la-la land, not paying attention and wishing stupid-ass LaVon was built like that and not the skinny stick that he was. So he smiled and nodded and I suddenly realized that I'd been gawking and that he had seen me. Aw, man, I hated looking like a fool, especially around cute guys.

First I tripped getting out of the car, then I got blasted by my grandmother on my vernacular and now I sat there staring probably with my tongue hanging out. Whatever. So he started to walk over, smiling like he knew something I didn't.

"Hey," he said, grinning with perfectly straight teeth and this serious deep dimple in the side of his face.

"Hey," I said, acting like I hadn't been staring him down.

"I haven't seen you around here before, you moving in with Mrs. King?" he asked.

"Yeah," I said, sparkling with conversation.

He nodded and leaned in. "Don't let her spook you, she acts cold and mean, but she's really not. It's the retired librarian still in her, I think. I've been doing her lawn and shoveling her snow for years, she's all right, you just have to get to know her."

I nodded, but the first thing I noticed when he talked was that he said the word all right and not a'ight. She must have gotten to him, too. "She's my grandmother."

"Really, then you're Jade's sister?" he asked.

"Cousin," I corrected him.

"Do you dance, too?"

"Yeah."

"At Freeman?"

Okay, that was enough. "What is this, twenty questions?" I asked, for some reason getting annoyed with him, but really annoyed with myself.

"Chill, shorty, I'm just asking."

"A'ight, then stop asking."

"What's up with you?" he asked with a seriously smug smirk on his face.

"I don't talk to strangers, okay," I said crisply, then looked away, back to the shed. He burst out laughing. I turned back to look at him. "What's so funny?"

"You sound just like Jade."

"Whatever, bye," I said dismissively.

He laughed again. "Yep, just like her."

"What is your problem?" I asked.

"I could ask you that same question."

We looked at each other, I glared, then rolled my eyes to look away and ignored him. He was too cute. "I saw you checking me out."

"I was not checking you out, I was looking at the shed," I said, lying my butt off, then I turned and looked at the shed again as if to reiterate my point.

"Yeah, right," he said obviously not believing me.

"Yeah, right," I repeated childishly, then looked back at him. He smiled. "So, are you and Jade together?" I kinda asked.

"Nah, she's out of my league. She's cool, though. She can dance her butt off."

Whatever, I thought but instead I nodded, having no idea why everybody kept saying that, 'cause as far as I could see, she was just cold and mean.

"So where did you say you were from?"

"I didn't say, goodbye."

"Oh, that's right, you didn't."

"You're like a cockroach, you just don't go away."

He laughed. "Did you go to the Tyrece Grant video shoot?"

"More questions," I said, and he smiled and chuckled again. It was kinda nice hearing him laugh. "Yeah, I was there."

"I thought I saw you there," he said knowingly, then looked up behind me and smiled. "You're all set, Mrs. King. The hostas and astilbes are getting thick behind the shed, and you should check your roses on the side of the house, they're a little buggy. It looks like there's something going on there."

I turned around and saw my grandmother standing at the back door looking out. She had an apron on now as she smiled and nodded. "Thanks, baby, I noticed that and picked up some spray earlier," she said.

"Cool, I'll take care of it tomorrow."

"That'll be fine."

"Anything else you need?" he asked her.

"No, I'll see you tomorrow."

"Yes, ma'am," he said, then he looked back at me and said, "See you later, shorty, take care."

"Bye," I said, then watched as he went down the short path, then around to the side of the house. He turned once, smiled, then kept going. He obviously knew I'd be watching him.

"Kenisha, do me a favor and go tell your mother dinner is almost ready, and while you're upstairs make sure those movers put everything exactly the way you wanted it. I believe they're still around here somewhere, so don't be shy about speaking your mind and telling them what you want. Your mother's paying them good money, so they need to put everything exactly where you want it."

"Yes, ma'am," I heard myself saying, mimicking the lawn mower guy, then stood to follow her back inside. I went into the kitchen and smelled something seriously good then I headed to the front of the house then upstairs.

I went to my room and saw a ton of boxes already there, piled on the floor against the wall. My bed was put together, along with my dresser and my computer table.

It was strange looking around and seeing all my stuff there like this. It was my room all over again but different. I'm not saying I liked it, but it could have been worse.

My mom was already in my bedroom and she apparently got the movers to put everything in place. She was looking out the window when I walked in.

"I remember this view being incredible when I was young. I would sit here for hours just looking out at the different houses. Being the four-corner area, the houses are all so varied, singles next to row next to twins next to what could be mansions. I guess back in the eighteen-hundreds it didn't matter what kind of house you had."

"Grandmom said that dinner is almost ready and that I should make sure that the movers put everything in place."

She turned to me, then looked around the room and nodded silently. "The movers just left. I think this will do fine. What do you think, how do you like it, nice, huh?"

"Yeah, it's nice," I said, looking around again.

"Kind of looks like your old bedroom, doesn't it?"

"But it's not," I said, feeling myself getting mad.

"No, it's not," she said then paused. "We should go downstairs, your grandmother cooked something special. I told her how much you like fried chicken, so she made an early dinner for us."

"So this is it. I have to stay here and that's it. I don't get a say in my life or nothing."

"Or anything."

"Whatever. I can't believe this, this is so wrong and you know it. You decided that that's it and I don't even get a say. You walk out and drag me with you. Now I'm stuck here to do what? No friends, no boyfriend."

"Kenisha, don't start. Look, I'm sorry your life didn't work like you expected, but neither did mine. I didn't expect to have to move back in with my mother at this age, but I have no choice."

"You have a choice, you just didn't take it. We can still go back."

"No," she said, taking a deep breath. "I made a choice long ago and now I have to live with it. I'm only sorry that you and Jade have to, too. And I'm not discussing this with you anymore."

"See, that's what I'm talking about. You don't even want to discuss it. Like what I say doesn't even matter."

"I didn't say that and I'm not going to argue with you. I'm tired and you just need to get used to this so come on, dinner is ready."

She walked out. That was it.

So then I was sitting there trying to figure out what had happened to my perfect life. A few minutes later I went downstairs to the kitchen table that was seriously spread out—fried chicken, potato salad, collard greens and cornbread.

Everybody was already seated. Jade was there. I sat between her and my mom. Jade reached out and took my hand, as did my Mom and Grandmom. They bowed their heads, I did, too, and Grandmom said a prayer of thanks pretty much centered around Mom and me being there.

With my head bowed I wasn't sure I should have been thankful for it. I didn't ask for it and I don't want it. We don't exactly go to church, but still I offered a request to have everything back the way it should be. Just in case.

So we started eating and everything was fine. Mom and my grandmom were talking about the neighborhood and Jade was saying something, but I didn't say anything.

"I hope you like your room, Kenisha," my grandmom said.

"Yeah," I said, then corrected myself. "Yes, it's nice."

"Good. If you need anything or can't find something, just ask Jade. I'm sure she'll be happy to help out."

"Okay," I said, but got the feeling that I was on my own. I noticed that Jade didn't say anything after that. As a matter of fact, she said very little throughout dinner. Mom and my grandmother kept talking about the good ol' days, when she had lived there, but me and Jade were just eating. I guess we both couldn't care less.

After dinner I went into the living room while my mom, Jade and my grandmother stayed and cleaned up the kitchen. I was standing there looking at the old photos on the wall, trying to see if there was a family resemblance or if they were just old photos on the wall.

"Your past becomes your future." I turned around; my grandmother was there beside me. "Remember that," she said.

"What does it mean?" I asked her.

"It means that once you've witnessed someone standing on a live land mine, you should be leery of repeating the action."

"So don't stand on live land mines?" I asked.

"No. Well, yes, that, too," she said, then smiled. I was

shocked. I swear it was the first time I'd actually seen the woman show any kind of emotion other than anger or frustration. "It means seeing someone else's mistake should hinder you from repeating it."

"Oh, I get it. Where'd you learn that?"

"Pearls of wisdom from many years of experience."

I nodded, then turned back to the photos on the wall.

"That's my great aunt, your great-great-great-aunt Harriet. She roamed the globe, married, divorced, then married a few more times. She spent most of her life running away but never really going anywhere. And that's Julia, her older sister, born at the turn of the last century, in the year 1900, worked all her life till the day she died, penniless. That's Anna Mae, she was a civil rights activist in the sixties, a real hell-raiser who spent more time in jail than out, and that's your great-great-uncle Lawrence. I don't know a lot about him other than the fact that he was married to a woman named Pearl. He walked away from her and six kids and no one heard a word since."

"That's so sad, why do you keep their photos on the wall if they were all so...tragic?"

"Land mines to future generations, but know this, appearances aren't always what you see."

I nodded, then moved over to the next photo of a young girl with two long, thick braids, sitting alone against the backdrop of a painted landscape. She looked timid and nervous, but mostly she looked sad. Dressed in a nautical outfit with a wide white collar, she held her hands clasped tightly together in her lap. "Who's that?" I asked.

"That's Vivian, she was the youngest, also your great-great-great-aunt. She died at sixteen of a leaking heart."

"A leaking heart, I never heard of that, what is it?"

"I don't know," she said, frowning.

"She looks just like Mom."

"Yes, she does, especially around the eyes."

I looked closer into her eyes. My grandmother was right, they had the same sadness in their eyes. Unmistakable.

"I have more photos if you're interested."

"No, but maybe later," I said, not in the mood to see more tragic family photos.

She nodded, then walked away. I had seriously gotten depressed, so I decided to go outside and take a look around. It was late afternoon, but kids were still outside playing in the street. I stood and watched them, thinking how good it would be to be back home, where I belonged.

"Why don't you go for a walk?" my mom said, standing behind me.

"Nah, maybe later," I said and just stood there.

"You okay?" she asked.

"Yeah, great, fine," I said. She turned to leave, but I stopped her. "Mom," I said. She turned back to me. "I'm sorry, I'm just…" I said.

"I know, I'm just, too…"

"So, Grandmom's photos on the wall, what's with them?"

"Family."

"Yeah, I know that part, but why, if they all lived such tragic lives, why display them on the wall like that?"

"Tragic to us, but not to them."

"What do you mean?"

"As one of the few black female pilots in her time, Harriet traveled the world and experienced more things than we can possibly imagine. Julia worked hard, amassed a fortune, then, having no children, gave all of it away to a children's charity before she died. They renamed it after her."

"Wow, I didn't know that."

"Anna Mae marched with Dr. King for our civil rights and was one of the few female Panthers, and Lawrence, well, I have no idea about him. But there is greatness in our family, remarkable women who stood above their challenges."

"Grandmom said that they were land mines, like lessons to be learned from their lives."

"In a way they are. What looks like something tragic might also be someone's victory. We can't always see that right away."

"Like you leaving Dad?"

She didn't say anything, but we both knew that she didn't have to. I smiled, feeling better, then started chuckling. "You know at first, after talking to Grandmom, I thought I came from a family of nuts."

Mom reached out and hugged me. It felt good. "You do."

We laughed and for the first time in days I felt okay.

"You know Freeman is about four or five blocks down."

"It's that close?" I asked.

"Yep, why don't you go over for a while, loosen up?"

"What about my punishment?"

"Let's call this a clean slate."

I nodded. It was the best idea I'd heard all day. Having

not danced in almost two weeks because of being grounded, it would feel good to get back out onto the boards again.

A half hour later I was walking into the building. I went to the office and signed out one of the private dance classrooms on the top floor. I turned on my music and started stretching, then I did one of my old routines just to feel the movement and work out any stiffness.

Afterwards I worked on my latest dance routine, then made some changes, incorporating a few steps I'd seen the other night. I watched myself in the mirror and saw that it was working, so I started again from the top.

It felt good to be back on the floor again. Dancing always made me feel free and alive and I knew that nothing bad could happen when I danced. As soon as I finished the routine, I heard applause and looked around.

"Not bad, shorty."

It took me a second to figure out who it was, lawn mower guy. "What are you doing here, you following me or something?"

He laughed and that stupid dimple flashed at me. "Nah, I came to drop off my little cousins. Are you always this paranoid?"

"Always," I said, just in case he got any ideas.

"I guess that's because of where you grew up. My guess is some snobbish neighborhood in Maryland or Virginia."

"You need to chill on that, okay, 'cause you don't know anything about me."

"I know you're not from around here anywhere."

"Duh…you saw me move in."

"Unless of course you are and you're just naturally stuck up."

"For your information, I grew up as far away from here as possible."

"It shows."

"Excuse me?"

"It shows," he repeated louder.

"I heard you the first time, I just didn't think you had nerve enough to repeat it. And for your information, I am not stuck-up."

"My mistake," he said, and smiled, obviously enjoying the prickly conversation.

"Exactly, now if you don't mind."

He started laughing again. "You're something else, you know that?"

"Yeah, I've been told."

"I like it," he said.

I tried hard not to grin or show any emotion, but something inside smiled. "Whatever, do you mind?"

"No, not at all, help yourself," he said, then walked over to the only furniture, a desk and chair in the far corner, and dropped his book. "You won't disturb me, unless of course you have the music up too loud."

"I'm asking you to leave," I said, then looked at him hard like he was some kind of moron or something.

"Sorry, but this is my room and my time, shorty."

"What?"

"I reserved this studio," he said.

"No way, I reserved this studio for one hour, hence the

words, private dance studio," I said, then walked over to the desk, stepping up to him.

"That's all well and good, but time's up, sweetheart," he said, nodding up at the clock over the door.

I looked up at the clock. He was right. I'd been dancing and as usual lost track of time. I'd reserved the studio for an hour and I was already ten minutes over.

"I'm not finished."

"Too bad, go next door, it's empty."

"Why don't you go next door?" I said.

"The light's better in here," he said, looking at the early-evening sun streaming through the uncovered windows.

"Light for what?" I asked, glancing down at the book on the desk, trying to read the cover.

"It doesn't matter for what," he said, losing the joyous lilt in his tone, then guardedly picking up the book and holding it to his side. "The point is I reserved it and your time is up."

"Do you dance?" I asked.

"Nah, not really."

"So why do you need the studio?"

"Again, doesn't matter, it's reserved."

"Fine," I said as amicably as I could, then marched over, grabbed up my bag and empty water bottle, then left. I was getting tired anyway.

Having not seriously danced in weeks, my body had stiffened, and having not done my usual stretching afterwards, I was really stiff by the time I walked back to my grandmother's house. I took a hot shower and relaxed.

The rest of the evening was quiet. I stayed in my room and watched TV and chilled out mostly. I tried calling my dad and LaVon again, but neither one was picking up, haters. I called Jalisa.

"Hey, how'd it go?" she asked as soon as she picked up the phone.

"Okay, fine, I'm here."

"How is it?"

"It's all right, noisy sometimes."

"Did you catch up with your dad?"

"No, not yet. I left another message."

"He'll call you back. Are you going to dance class on Monday afternoon?"

"Yeah, my punishment's been reprieved."

"I know you can't wait to get back to dancing."

"It's actually just a few blocks away. I can walk there in a few minutes. As a matter of fact, I was just there this afternoon."

"Wow, no more Metro train and Union Station, I'm seriously jealous."

"You should stop by Monday and check it out. My bedroom looks just like it did before. But check, the house is as old as the Pyramids. It's like an antique warehouse."

"Cool, I will, although I can't stay long, I have to work Monday night. You talk to LaVon lately?" she asked.

"Nah, I tried calling him a few minutes ago, he's not picking up. I'm getting seriously tired of his drama. He's always acting like he all that, wanna be a player and he's got all these hard-up skanks on his tail and loving it. He so full of it, his drama is played and I'm seriously ready to blow him off."

My second line beeps. It was LaVon. So I hung up with Jalisa and picked up.

"Hey, I was gonna call you," he said first thing.

"Whatever," I said.

"What, you don't believe me?"

"Can we not do this, okay?"

"Not do what?" he asked, as if he didn't know.

"Nothing, never mind."

"Yo, I'm cool, you acting all stressed and all."

"So what's up? What you doing tonight?" I asked, hoping that he'd come and keep me company my first night there.

"Chilling, you know how I do."

"Why don't you come over and hang out."

"Where you at?"

"At my grandmom's house."

"In D.C.?"

"Yeah, in D.C."

"I ain't driving all the way to D.C., shorty."

"Why not? You drive your butt over here all the time," I said, then I heard muffled voices and he covered the phone to say something to somebody there with him. "What, you got company?" I asked.

"Check, shorty, some of my boys just came by, I'll holler at you later."

"What?"

"I gotta go."

"I called to talk to you and you gonna go 'cause your

boys are there. What's up with that? Never mind." I hung up.

I lay across the bed trying to decide if I should call my dad again. Then I heard Jade in her room with music on, then her talking to someone on the phone. Then a few minutes later I heard her going downstairs. I guess I fell asleep 'cause it was the last thing I remember.

CHAPTER 10

Dealing with New Drama

"This merry-go-round is getting monotonous, up and down, round and round. I keep getting knocked down by the same drama over and over again, time for something new."

—*myspace.com*

I fell asleep in my clothes.

I was in a different room in a different house in a different city and state, almost state. I got up, grabbed a quick shower and got ready to start my day. Of course I had no idea what I was supposed to be doing now. Talk about a fish out of water.

Anyway, I went downstairs to check what was happening. I figured maybe I'd sit outside awhile, but just as I decided to do that, my cell rang. I checked the number before I answered. If it was LaVon, I was gonna cuss him out. It wasn't LaVon.

I answered. "What."

"Kenisha."

"Yeah, what?"

"That's not the greeting I expected."

"Too bad," I muttered under my breath.

"You need to correct your tone and your attitude."

Tsst, I sucked my teeth, seriously not in the mood to listen to his parental crap. "Oh, please," I muttered again, this time loud enough for him to clearly hear me.

"As I said, that's not the greeting I expected."

"And this isn't the bedroom I expected, but I have to deal with it, don't I?"

"I know this is difficult for you to understand, but it was for the best."

"Best for who, you?"

"Your mother and I needed this time apart. We need to reevaluate our relationship and come to some reasonable conclusions. We had choices to make, they weren't easy, but they needed to be made."

"Uh-huh." I hummed, sounding disinterested.

"I'm sorry if the decisions we made are unacceptable to you."

"Whatever," I said, already tired of listening to his trash-talking.

"Watch your mouth, young lady, I'm still your father."

"Since when?" I asked. He went quiet for a while.

"We need to talk," he finally said.

"Are we moving back home?" I asked.

"That won't be possible."

"Then what do we have to talk about?" I hung up. His drama was getting old. That smooth-talking crap might have worked for those stupid women he surrounded himself with at work, but it didn't fly with me. He was my father, yes, so big deal. My cell phone rang again. It was him. I just let it ring.

I went downstairs to see what was going on in the kitchen, since I started smelling this awesome aroma. I didn't know what it was, but it started to make my stomach grumble. I found my mom sitting in the kitchen, drinking tea and flipping through the Sunday newspaper. "Good morning," she said.

"Morning," I said, then looked around for my grandmother or Jade.

"Momma and Jade went to church. We'll be going with them next week. I thought you might want to sleep in this morning. Are you hungry?"

I nodded, realizing that I was. My stomach wasn't growling or anything, but I could serious eat something.

My mom got up and went over to the refrigerator and pulled out a dozen eggs, orange juice and some bread. I went over to the stove and check to see if the water in the teapot was still hot. It was. So I turned and looked around for a cup.

"The second cabinet on the left," she said, "first shelf right in front of you. Tea bags are in the cabinet next to them on the right."

So I got a cup and poured myself a cup of water, then added a tea bag and sugar, then sat at the table and started flipping through the same newspaper my mom had.

"How'd you sleep?" she asked, adding bacon and sausage to my plate.

"A'ight, sorry, fine, I slept fine," I said, correcting myself and realizing that I was almost lying 'cause I completely knocked out last night. I didn't even remember turning off the light. I remembered falling asleep and hearing voices, I think I heard my mom talking to Jade.

"Good," she said as she cracked two eggs into a frying pan and began to scramble then.

"How'd you sleep?" I asked her.

"Okay," she said.

"I think I heard you talking to Jade last night." She looked at me. "I don't get it, what's up with her?"

"What do you mean?"

"She's always pissed, at least with me she acts pissed."

"What makes you say that?"

"Did I do something to her?"

She paused a second before answering. "No."

"So what is it, then?"

"Jade didn't have the advantages you had growing up, so give her a break, okay?"

"You mean kiss her butt."

"I mean, give her a break. It's not easy living here."

"I heard you say that you were proud of her."

"I am, I'm very proud of her, I'm proud of both of you. Do you have any plans for today?"

"No, not really, I guess I'll unpack some boxes, then I might check out the neighborhood, go for a walk and look around."

"Just be careful," she said as she finished with my eggs, and the toast popped up just as she poured a glass of juice. I ate, listening to her talk about the good old days and how it was when she was growing up around there. "You know your grandfather was a preacher."

I look up, interested for the first time. "Where?"

"The same church Momma and Jade attend." She smiled and shook her head. "They loved him there, the man could do no wrong."

She stopped talking and just started staring. It was strange. "So he died, right?"

She nodded. "He was killed coming home from church one night. The neighborhood almost rioted trying to find the fool who stabbed him for twenty-six dollars and nineteen cents. The thing was, he would have given the money up anyway. He was like that, always giving to someone else. His time, his patience, his love..." There was something in her voice that didn't sound convincing, but I just let it go.

Jade and my grandmother came home from church about an hour later. I was back in my room by then, going through my stuff. I looked up just as Jade walked past my open door on her way down the hall to her bedroom. She didn't say anything and neither did I.

Seriously, I had no idea what her problem was. She walked around the house, coming and going like she was queen of the universe. No one said anything to her and her snarly, condescending and uppity attitude was really getting on my last nerve.

Jalisa called, we talked awhile, but still no LaVon. I was organizing my CDs when my cell rang again. It was my dad.

"I'm sending a cab for you this evening. I want you to have dinner with me here, we need to talk," he said.

Usually it was no big deal for my dad to take just me to dinner. We did it a lot. But I seriously wasn't in the mood to deal with him right then. He talked more and I finally agreed, then I went back to emptying boxes. Around five o'clock I showered, changed my clothes and went downstairs to wait for the cab.

"Where do you think you going?" my mom asked.

"Dad is sending a cab for me. He wants us to have dinner at the house tonight," I said, "to talk."

"Oh, really, when did all this happen?"

"He called a few hours ago," I said.

"And you're just finding time to tell me this now?"

"It's no big deal."

"Hell, yeah, it's a big deal, you're not going," she said sharply.

"I told him I would."

"Then tell him you're not. You're not going back to that house."

"Mom, I want to go, I want to hear what he has to say."

"No," she said adamantly, and turned her head.

"So what, you're just gonna keep me locked up here in this house for the rest of my life? I can't go anywhere just in case I might run into him or by some chance I see him in the street? What am I supposed to do if he calls me again, hang up on him?"

"I didn't say that. You can't go to that house. You tell him to have your meeting someplace else."

"It's already set for the house, he's cooking."

"Your father doesn't even know we had a kitchen. Believe me, he's not cooking."

"Okay, then, he's ordering out or something, what's the big deal? We ordered out for dinner all the time."

"Change it."

"Fine, I'll have the cab take me to a restaurant, he can meet me there."

"Call him now and set it up."

I called and got his voice mail. I left a message that I'd meet him at the restaurant off the parkway around the corner from the house. "Is that better?"

"Don't stay too long and don't even think about going over to that boy's house."

A car horn blew outside. I looked out the window; there was a cab in front of the house. "I have to go, bye," I said. She looked at me and nodded without saying anything. So I went outside and hopped in and he took off. Thank God. I was sick of this already. I turned around to see my mom standing on the front porch.

We got there quicker then I expected 'cause there wasn't a lot of traffic late Sunday afternoon. We pulled up in front of the house and I sat there waiting, looking up at my old house.

"This is it right?" the cabbie asked in broken English.

"Yeah," I said, "how much?" I asked, opening up my purse to get my credit card.

"It's already taken care of," he said.

I nodded, but I still didn't move. I saw the cabbie glance at me in the rearview mirror. "Thanks," I said, then finally opened the door and got out.

So now I was back home, my real home, where I wanted to be. I walked up the front steps and the first thing I saw was that my dad had obviously moved back into the house, 'cause there were curtains at the windows again and new front door knobs had been put back on to replace the ones my mom took when we left. I walked up and used my front door key to get in, but it didn't work. I rang the bell.

Dad opened the door, smiling at me. I looked at him like he was crazy. What in the world did he have to be smiling about? He started talking all nervous and all like he wanted to say something but didn't. I got ready to head upstairs when he told me to come into the living room and sit down like I was company or something.

In one day there was new furniture already. But it was cheap and flashy like it was picked up at some cheesy bargain basement place. Okay, I knew my mom had designed and decorated the house before, but I had always assumed that my dad had some kind of taste. I guess I was wrong.

"I'm glad you came," he said, crunching the cheap material as he sat down.

"So you want to tell me what this is all about?" I asked, getting right to the point before he started his trash-talking.

"You look good," he said, stalling.

"Thanks."

"I can't believe you're getting so grown, look at you, you're like a young lady now. I'm so proud of you."

"Then what did I do?" I asked.

"What do you mean, do what?"

"I must have done something for you to kick me out."

"No, nothing, sweetheart, you didn't do anything."

"So what was this about?"

"Your mother didn't tell you?"

"No."

"Then you should ask her."

"Mom's not talking, so I'm asking you," I said.

He took a deep breath and sighed long. My dad hated confrontations, so usually my mom covered for him. That's why he always had my mom tell me bad news, like that was gonna separate him from it and make him blameless or something. "People change, they grow apart, and your mother and I grew apart."

"I guess I grew apart from you, too, huh?"

"It's not like that, Kenisha."

"Then what is it like? I don't understand. Fine, you and Mom break up, separate, divorce, whatever, why can't I still live here with you?"

"It's just not possible."

"Why not?"

"Because it's not," he said firmly.

"Okay, so what about school next month?"

"Don't worry, I'll take care of everything."

"No, Dad, that's not good enough, I want to come home."

"I'm sorry, baby, but that's not possible, at least not right now. Maybe in a while you can come and spend the night or something."

"Spend the night, what's with that?" I asked.

"How's your mother?" he asked, changing the subject.

"Ask her," I said.

"How's your mother, Kenisha?"

"Fine, taking sleeping pills, muscle relaxers, anxiety pills, whatever, you know the drill."

"Listen, Kenisha, there are a few files I'm gonna need that were left in my office here. Your mother must have packed them, I need them back."

"Talk to her."

"I can't do that," he said. I shrugged. "Also, I was told that you had my client list on your laptop. I need that back, too."

"What client list on my laptop?"

"You know what I'm talking about."

"Not really, if you need something, you need to talk to Mom. She packed everything."

"That's not good enough," he said, then started talking this psychobabble stuff and I wasn't really listening, then he stopped and looked behind me. I turned around.

"Kenisha, you remember Courtney, don't you?" he said.

I looked at her standing there smugly with a Betty Crocker apron tied around her fat waist and a string of pearls around her neck and all of the sudden it made sense. She was the new woman in his life. We got put out of our house because of her.

"Oh, no, you didn't bring this skank in here," I said, standing with my hands on my hips. She was standing there with this big-ass stomach, smiling at me. I started over to her, but my dad grabbed me back, blocking between us 'cause I was ready to get busy on her ass. Truth was I had never fought a day in my life, but then, that day, that minute, I was seriously ready to step up on her.

"Excuse me, what did you just call me?" Courtney asked.

"You heard me," I said, leaning around my dad.

"Listen, little girl, it wasn't my idea to bring your ass back here tonight. If it was left up to me, you'd be…" she started, then stopped when my dad turned around to her.

"What?" I said, "if it were left up to you, what?"

"You need to show some respect," she finally said.

"Respect. Who, you, are you joking? You spread your legs for him, break my family up, move into my house and I need to show some respect for you? Please."

"My being here don't have nothing to do with you, and for your information, I didn't break up anything that wasn't already broke," she snapped back.

"What are you, a moron? This is my house, I live here."

"Correction, this is my house, I live here now."

"Skank," I said, ready to kick her ass again.

"You want some of me, come on. You need to step off, you and your crazy-ass pill-popping momma," she said, taking her apron off and throwing it on the floor.

"That's enough," my dad said, pulling my arm and holding me back. I looked at him and laughed. He must have been kidding. He actually moved this skank into my house and kicked me out. So I was about to tear that place up and kick her back to wherever she came from. "Kenisha, stop it."

"Me stop it, what about her?"

"Yes, Kenisha, you need to calm yourself down," Courtney said teasingly.

"Skank."

"Kenisha," he said firmly.

"What?" I looked at him like he was insane.

"Courtney, would you please give me a minute with my

daughter?" he said over his shoulder. She didn't move. He turned to her. "Please, please."

"Why do I have to go, she's the one acting all stupid, make her leave," she said, glaring at me steadily.

"Just check on dinner, please," he said.

She sucked her teeth and grabbed up the apron, then stomped back through the dining room. I rolled my eyes. I couldn't believe this was happening. My dad actually kicked me and my mom out for her.

"Come on, sit down," he said to me after she left.

I didn't move. I just stood there with my arms crossed over my chest, waiting for him to make this right.

"Look, Kenisha, this thing is between your mom and me. This has nothing to do with you or with Courtney, do you understand?"

"Nothing to do with me," I repeated. "In case you haven't noticed, I'm living in D.C. now."

"You need to be with your mother, and Courtney and I need some time alone to be together. I'll bring you back, I swear, but not right now. I need to do this for me, for all of us." I started shaking my head. The bogus nobility of his crap was too pathetic.

"I know this is painful and confusing for you right now, but in a few weeks, you'll understand. What I did, I did for you. I love you and in a way I still love your mother, but I'm not in love with her. We needed to go our separate ways. It was time."

I just stared at him for a long time as he talked. He was such a cliché. "I can't believe you. You're like some sick joke, trading down. Can't you see she's just using you?"

"Kenisha, stop it." He raised his voice.

"No, better idea," I said calmly, "you stop it. You put Mom and me out for her. She's just a few years older than me, and you gave me drama when I wanted to date? But it's okay for you to screw her?"

"You don't judge me, I'm your father!" he yelled. "This is my life and I'm entitled to be happy. Courtney makes me happy. You're too young and inexperienced to understand all this."

"Oh, I'm too young," I said. "Okay, since I'm too young, I'll get experience. I'll go out and find me a fifty-year-old man like Courtney and then maybe I might just understand."

"Stop it, you're my child."

"She's somebody's child."

"That's none of your business." He paused and looked at me, realizing that I wasn't buying his crap. "Maybe you'd better leave. I'll call you a cab."

"Don't bother," I said, already heading to the front door.

"Kenisha, wait, Kenisha," he called out, but I just kept walking. "Kenisha, Courtney told me that you have a list of my clients on your computer. I need it back." I started laughing. As far as I was concerned, this Jerry Springer show was over.

CHAPTER 11

An Unexpected Ally

"When a perfect life turns out to be anything but and everything you thought was true isn't and the road back to where you want to be turns out to be all uphill, I guess you have to push pause and just start climbing."

—*myspace.com*

MY dad always had issues about getting older. He did everything in his power to act and fake being young. He talked it, dyed his hair, listened to more rap music than I did, drove a pimped-out ride and dressed like he was eighteen, baggy low-riding jeans and all. He tried to play basketball with the young guys, but he couldn't keep up and just made a fool of himself. He always had young women circling around him, so now he had this young skank on his arm and he thought that his life was complete. Wrong.

I decided to walk over to Jalisa's house a block away. She wasn't there. Natalie said that she was at work.

"You okay, girl?" she asked.

"Yeah," I said, starting to get frustrated and filled up, but I refused to let the tears come again. "I just stopped by to say hey."

"Listen, I'm on my way to work, so I can drop you off at the mall or at Jalisa's job if you want. You can get your mom to pick y'all up afterwards."

"Okay."

She grabbed her purse and we got into her car. She started talking about catching up with my mom, and I realized that she had no idea we had moved out. Jalisa had never told her. So she talked, but before I was supposed to reply, her cell rang and she picked up.

Thank God. 'Cause I seriously was not in the mood to deal with Natalie. So she was talking on the cell and driving and we drove past LaVon's house. I was just about to tell Natalie to pull over and let me out, but then I saw Chili's car in the driveway.

Okay, I knew that Chili had a thing for LaVon's older brother, but as far as I knew he was in the military and stationed in New Jersey or New Mexico or something like that. So what was Chili's car doing there?

But by the time it occurred to me to tell Natalie to pull over, she was already down the block and around the corner. Natalie drove fast. So I figured I'd call Chili and find out what's up with that later.

So we got to the mall and Jalisa was there working. She wasn't off for another hour and a half, so I decided to just hang around and wait. I called Chili, but she wasn't answering. I called LaVon again. He picked up.

"I was just gonna call you," he said as usual.

"So why didn't you?"

"You know how it is," he said.

"How's Chili?"

"She a'ight, I guess," he said, then tried to cover. "Why you asking me, how am I supposed to know?"

"I went by your house a few minutes ago and I thought I saw her car parked out front."

"Nah, that was my boy's car. He stopped by to check out the game. We just chilling."

"Uh-huh."

"What, you don't believe me?" he asked.

"I didn't say that."

"So you just gonna 411 and get all up in my grill."

"Just bump it," I said, annoyed that I'd even called him.

"So you moved, right," he said, rather than asked.

"Yeah, yesterday, it went okay."

"How's D.C.?"

"It's all right, my grandmother's house is small. It's old, real old, serious wood everywhere, the good stuff, and it's got three stories and this huge backyard. My bedroom is on the third floor and from the window you can see almost ten blocks away 'cause it's the tallest house in the neighborhood. You should stop by and check it out."

"Check out your grandmother's house, nah, pass on that."

I smiled and chuckled to myself, remembering the one time LaVon met my grandmother, like, three years ago at my birthday party and she almost smoked him. She embarrassed the mess out of him right in front of his boys. It was a trip. His boys bounced on him about that for weeks, threatening to call her whenever he acted up. "You still scared of my little old grandmother?"

"I ain't scared of nobody, I just don't want to deal with that D.C. traffic."

"Oh, please, you go to D.C. all the time."

"Why you stressing me out about this, it's not like we gonna do anything if I do show up. So what's the big deal?"

"What?"

"Yeah, a'ight, whatever," he said, obviously getting distracted by something or someone.

"So you still have company?" I asked, but he didn't reply. "LaVon, LaVon."

"What?" he said.

"Nothing."

"Yo, let me check you later," he said.

"That's all right, I gotta go anyway, but why don't you come over to the mall later. I'm waiting for Jalisa to get off in an hour and we can hang out."

"Huh? Yeah, what?"

I hung up. Like my dad, his trash-talking was getting old, too.

So I was sitting there in the food court pissed off when Diamond walked up and stopped at my table. She stood there with all these bags and I looked up at her.

"Hey," Diamond said.

"Hey," I said.

"I heard about you moving," she said. What, did everybody know now? "Chili told a friend of mine. Sorry."

"About what?"

"Your mom and dad."

I need to seriously shut Chili's big mouth up. "Yeah, whatever."

"Can I sit down?" she asked.

I seriously wasn't in the mood for more drama, so I just waved my hand. I didn't care anymore. She sat down.

"Look, it's not me. You were my girl since we were four years old in dance class. So you talking this about me and LaVon is wrong, you need to look someplace else with that."

I just nodded absently. I really didn't feel like dealing with all that right now. She shrugged, then stood up, grabbing up her bags.

"What'd you get?" I asked her, deciding that I didn't want to be sitting in the food court alone.

She stopped and held up a bag. "A top, a belt and some jeans."

"At Urban Chic?" I asked, seeing the logo on the bag.

She nodded. "Yeah, they just got some nice things in."

"Let me see what you got," I said. She pulled out the top and the belt and I checked it out. Diamond always did have nice taste. At one time she talked about being a fashion buyer. I could seriously see her doing it. She pulled out her jeans and they were the same ones I'd bought a week ago, before any of this happened. It seemed like years ago now. "I just got these, too," I said.

"Oh, yeah."

I nodded. "They fit tight, but they're nice. I like the designs on the pockets."

"That was why I got them," she said.

"I like their new window displays."

"Me, too, they have this one on the side. It's like a photo shoot with the mannequin wearing this green top…"

"…with the gray belt and burgundy designs," I jumped in, finishing her thought just like always.

"Yeah, that's the one, I love that outfit, but…"

"…never buy window display," we said in unison, then smiled and laughed. It felt good to laugh with Diamond again.

"So are you waiting for Jalisa to get off?" she asked.

"Yeah," I said, then looked at my cell to check the time. I still had another forty minutes.

She nodded. "I'm gonna stop by that new shoe store on the corner. You want to come with? I mean, I understand if you don't, it's okay, I mean…"

I stood up. "Sure, let's go."

So we walked the mall and at first it was strange but we were talking and it was all awkward and all, then we started joking around, playing, laughing and talking about people and then I hardly remembered why we'd stopped being friends. Then I remembered Chili and Diamond had this huge argument one day after Chili's boyfriend dumped her and tried to talk to Diamond. Everybody got pissed at Diamond, including me. That was when everybody started saying that Diamond would screw anybody's boyfriend. Her rep sank just like that.

But most girls didn't like Diamond anyway 'cause most guys did like her. Diamond was seriously *America's Top Model, American Idol* and *Project Runway* all rolled into one. She wasn't just cute, she was open-mouth, staring in disbelief, drop-dead beautiful. But she didn't act it, so that was why they all hated her. They were all jealous. But I wasn't jealous, I was just pissed 'cause Chili told me that she was going after LaVon. I guess Chili was mistaken.

"I don't know if I'm going back to Hazelhurst."

"Why not?"

"You know my mom and I moved out," I said. She nodded. "We're living with my grandmother in D.C., so I might go to school there. If I do, I hope it's the one for art, music and dance like Jade. I heard she busted out big there."

"I like Jade, she was always cool."

"I don't know."

"What do you mean?"

"She acts funny with me, like I pissed her off or something. I have no idea what I did, but she is seriously hating on me."

"Did you ask her?"

"Nah," I said.

"You should ask her what's up."

"Like she'd tell me."

"She might," Diamond said.

So I started thinking. Maybe I should just talk to Jade and find out what's up.

"Chili told me that she saw you and LaVon together," I said, completely changing the subject.

"You were my girl, Kenisha, I would never do anything like that. Chili's lying."

I nodded 'cause after everything I started to see things differently. Jalisa was right, the three of us had been friends since we were four years old and I should have trusted that friendship and given Diamond the benefit of the doubt.

So my cell rang. It was Jalisa, she had just gotten off work. She walked down and met me and Diamond at the shoe store, then we checked out a few other stores, then we went back over to the food court and grabbed something to eat. It was late, so Diamond drove Jalisa home and took me to the Metro station so I could catch a train to D.C.

On the train I started thinking about everything. It was a screwed-up day from beginning to end. Tomorrow had to be better.

CHAPTER 12

My Eyes Wide Shut

"I see shadows now, gray and black shadows. I guess when you're blind, people expect you not to see. But what if you're not and you still can't see? I open my eyes and still see nothing."

—*myspace.com*

A few days went by without much drama. I spent most of the time either at Freeman's or in my new bedroom. I hadn't spoken to my dad and that was just fine with me 'cause he was on my last nerve anyway. He did leave me a few messages on my cell to tell me that he wanted me to get my mom to drop off those papers he'd left in his office and for me to return the client list on my laptop. He had to be kidding, like that was actually going to happen.

First of all, all that stuff was packed up, sitting in some huge storage bin in Virginia, and if he wanted his client list, then he needed to come correct and step up.

I hadn't spoken to LaVon since that night at the mall, on the phone. It was his senior year at Kentwood Prep and he had basketball practice all the time, so I guess he was supposed to be focusing on that. I didn't really care about that, either.

Since I was usually in my bedroom in the morning and out in Virginia in the afternoon, then back late, I hadn't actually seen my mom since I talked to her the night I met with my dad. She stayed in her bedroom mostly. I heard crying one time when I passed by and one time I heard her in there talking to Jade about something. I kept on going.

Jade was nothing like I'd remembered. I knew everybody said how cool she was but I wasn't seeing any of that. We shared the third floor, but we didn't talk and she was gone most of the time anyway.

Although, since I was up early this morning, I bumped into her. She was in the closet and the door to her side of the bathroom was open. "Morning," I said, then looked in the mirror and pulled my hair back with a clip, then picked up my toothbrush and toothpaste.

"Good morning," she said, about to leave the closet to go back into her bedroom.

"You know we should talk, maybe," I said.

"About what?" she asked.

"I don't know, anything, whatever."

She looked at me. "Fine, we just did."

"No, I mean for-real talk."

"I have to go," she said, then looked at her watch as if

to make the point that she was too busy. "We can talk later." So that was that, the end of conversation.

So today I went downstairs and my grandmother was in the kitchen cooking, seemed like she was always cooking. It smelled good, though. I sat down, expecting to have our usual detached conversation, which usually ended up with her telling me that I needed to speak like an intelligent person, as she put it, and not like a street urchin. What in the world was a street urchin?

"Morning," I said as I walked in, sat down and grabbed a homemade blueberry muffin from a pyramidlike stack on a platter in the center of the kitchen table.

"Good morning," she said, then glanced up at the clock. It was a little after nine, way early for me.

I knew that was what she was thinking 'cause she gave me that look. I usually didn't come downstairs until noon, that way I didn't have to deal with anyone 'cause I knew Jade would be out someplace, my mom would be in her room still asleep and my grandmother would either be at church or in the yard with her plants. Today I just didn't feel much like sleeping in.

"I know you're not just going to sit there like that and not get over here and help me."

"I don't cook," I said, nibbling on the muffin.

"Didn't your mother teach you anything about cooking?"

"She cooks, we order in or we eat out. I can't cook."

"Good, that means you can learn. Come on over here."

I stood up slowly and went over to the stove. I watched her a minute while she stirred something in a huge silver pan. "Here, take this spoon and stir while I get some fresh herbs from the garden."

"Maybe I should get the herbs," I said, looking at the pale stuff she was stirring and having the feeling it would burn as soon as she walked away and left me alone with it.

"Do you know what rosemary, thyme, chives, parsley and basil look like?"

"No," I said.

"Then maybe you're better stay here and stir," she said simply, and left me just like that.

Okay....

So I stood there stirring this strange, tannish, palish looking stuff in this pan, and I looked around wondering what in the world I was doing there and when or if she was even coming back.

"Hey."

I turned and saw the lawn mower guy open the screen door carrying a grocery bag. He came in like he was one of the family. "Oh, man," I muttered under my breath, "this is all I need.

"Hey," I said barely audibly, still stirring.

"So you cook, huh?"

"Yeah, I cook," I said, lying, of course.

"What are you cooking?" he asked.

Oops. I looked down into the pan and for the first time realized that I had no idea what I was doing. So like a complete fool I just kept stirring. I swear I was gonna say something, but for some reason nothing came out.

"Cat got your tongue, or do you still not speak to strangers?" he asked.

"Who are you exactly, I mean, other than lawn mower guy?" I heard myself asking. "What are you, like, the handyman, babysitter or something? Do you live in the basement, the attic or the shed? 'Cause every time I turn around, you're here."

He laughed, then put the bags he was carrying down on the counter and walked over to see what I was doing. He leaned in and I could feel his breath tickle my neck. I shivered. "Try not to burn that," he whispered way too close.

"Yeah, thanks, lawn mower guy, see ya," I said, dismissing him again.

"Trying to get rid of me already?" he said, inching closer to me.

"Don't you have something else to do or someone else to mess with?"

"Yeah, but I like messing with you."

"Uh-huh, yeah, I got that part."

"So what are you doing later?" he asked.

"Don't you have a girlfriend or a boyfriend?"

He laughed again and made me want to laugh, too. "Nah, shorty, I don't even fly that side of the fence and as for the part about a girlfriend, not at the moment, you interested?"

"Sorry, I'm seeing someone."

"Ah, yes, the NBA wannabe…"

"What do you know about it and how do you know about LaVon anyway?"

"Life is transient."

"What's that supposed to mean?" I asked, turning around to face him.

Before I knew anything he leaned in and kissed me. I let him. It was nice, really nice, soft and firm but not demanding, like LaVon always was. Neither one of us moved an inch or touched anything other than our lips. I kept on stirring and he just stood there, too close. When he finally leaned back, he smiled all cocky, like he knew that was gonna happen. "I bet Mr. NBA don't even compare," he whispered.

"Bye," I said, dismissing him again and then I turned to look down, concentrating on the stuff I was still supposed to be stirring. But umm, he was sure-nuff right about LaVon's kiss not comparing to his.

"See you later, shorty," he whispered in my ear, then left.

As soon as the back door closed, I looked up. I didn't really expect him to leave like that. Before, when I said bye, he just kept on talking. So I walked over to the back door and looked out. I didn't see him anywhere, but I heard my grandmother talking, I guess to her next-door neighbor. I hurried back to the stove just in case she came back in. The last thing I needed to hear was her mouth. After about five minutes, my grandmother decided to come back in. I was still standing there, stirring.

"How's it look?" she asked.

"It got darker. I don't know, I guess I might have burned it or something. Sorry."

She came over and looked over my shoulder, then nodded. "It looks just fine, just keep stirring just like that."

"What is it?" I asked.

"It's a roux."

"What's a roux?"

"A roux is a base sauce. There are several variations. This one is made with flour and butter and just a hint of bacon drippings. You melt the butter, then slowly sprinkle the flour a little bit at a time then stir for about thirty minutes. The more you stir, the darker the roux and the more flavorful the base. But if you burn it, you have throw it out and start over."

"Oh, right." I nodded like I had the slightest clue what she was talking about. Then I watched as she started doing all this stuff, chopping, mixing, grating. I had no idea what she was making, but it was seriously smelling good.

"What's it gonna be?" I asked.

"It's going to be seafood gumbo."

"So you have all these recipes memorized or do you write them down in a cookbook?" I heard myself ask her.

"There are two types of recipes in this kitchen. The ones that feed the body and the ones that feed the soul. One set you'll find in cookbooks in the pantry, and the other you won't."

I smiled. "More pearls of wisdom," I said.

"Exactly. We all change the world in our way and just by being born you've changed it. But the recipe for making your own history is decide what you want, commit to your decision, then be able to live with the consequences. Follow your heart. It'll never let you down."

"Can I ask you something?"

"Sure."

"What's up with Jade?" I asked. She just looked at me. "I mean, why is she so quiet all the time, introverted?" I wanted to say evil, but I changed my mind and went with quiet and introverted instead.

"I presume you're asking why Jade seems distant."

"Yeah, I mean, yes. She acts okay around you and Mom, but with me she's all distant. Did I do something or say something to her?"

"Have you talked to her about this?"

"No. Well, yes, kind of. I tried, but she was distant again. She didn't want to hear me."

"Maybe you should try again, but this time make her hear you say something different. It's not always the way you say it but how you say it."

"She's in school still, right, college?"

"Yes, Howard University, going into her sophomore year," she said. I nodded. "Where do you intend to study?"

I shrugged. She looked at me hard. "I don't know yet," I said. "I was thinking about staying in the immediate area, but I haven't really decided yet."

"Have you taken the PSATs yet?"

"Yes, twice."

"How did you do?"

"I think I did okay."

"You think or you know?"

"I did okay."

"How are your grades?"

"I think they're okay."

"Why don't you try that answer again," she said.

Damn, I felt like I was getting the third degree in kindergarten. "I have a steady three-point-five GPA."

"Good, but a four-point-zero would be much better."

"Yes, I know. That was one of my goals this year."

"Good for you," she said. I was stunned. Did I actually get a "good for you" compliment? "Well, I think you might want to start considering your future, don't you?" I nodded. "Have you considered any specific schools yet or looked at college brochures?"

"No, I'm waiting until my junior year, this year."

"Don't wait too long," she said. I nodded for lack of anything else to do or say. "What are you interested in?"

"Ummm, I think I like computer engineering," I said, and then corrected myself. "I mean, I like computer engineering, I'm interested in that field." She smiled wide, then shook her head.

"What, you smiled. Why?"

"Your mother studied computer engineering before she met your father."

"Mom went to school for computer engineering?" I asked. "That's hot, I didn't know that."

"She had such promise."

"What do you mean had?"

"She didn't quite finish."

"Why not?"

"Maybe you should ask her."

I knew that was the end of that conversation, so I didn't even bother pressing her on the issue. As for asking my mom, I figured I'd think about it.

"Is Jade here?" I asked, wondering out loud.

"No, she's at work."

"Oh," I said, "where exactly does she work?"

"She works at the dance studio in the mornings and at the college library in the afternoons."

"I didn't know she actually worked there," I said, surprised.

"There's a lot you don't know. But be patient, you have a lot to learn."

I had no idea what that was supposed to mean, so I just nodded, figuring that was all I was gonna get.

"What are your plans for today?"

"Nothing," I said, figuring that I'd probably go to the mall in Virginia and catch up with my friends, then go to Freeman like usual.

"Good, I could use some help around the house and I need a few errands run."

"Me?" I stopped stirring.

"What, you too good to get your hands dirty?"

"No, I mean I don't know what to do."

"We'll show you."

"We'll?" I asked, curious as to who she was talking about.

"Don't stop stirring, I need that roux to be a nice dark brown." I nodded and looked at the sauce simmering in the pan. The color had darkened and deepened to a rich milk chocolate color.

My grandmother came over and looked over my shoulder again. "A little patience is all it takes to turn anything around, remember that."

I nodded. "Okay."

"Let me take that now," she said as I handed her the

spoon. "I need you to pick up a few things for me from the grocery store, then go down to the dance studio and find out what time Jade's coming back."

"Can't you just call her?"

She looked at me sternly. I got the message.

"Take my car. The keys are on the peg in the pantry."

"You want me to drive?"

"You know how, don't you?"

"Yeah, I mean yes, but it's just that…"

"Are you a good, safe driver?"

"Yes, definitely. I follow all the rules, pay attention to traffic, no cell phone…it's just that I have my learner's permit and all, but…"

"But what?" she asked.

"I need a real driver in the car with me."

"Take your time, drive carefully. You'll be fine and as for a licensed driver, it'll be our little secret," she said, then smiled and winked. "Now, is there anything else?"

Whoa, she winked, she smiled, hell must have just frozen over, I thought. "Uh, no, nothing, I need to get my purse," I said, and hurried up the stairs to my room. I went back down and grabbed the list and the keys from the pantry, then left.

My grandmother gave me a shopping list and directions, but I kept getting turned around, then I finally found the store she wanted. I parked and went inside and picked up all the things on her list. Having never gone grocery shopping before in my life, it took me forever, but I finally did it. So I was just about to get back in the car when I heard somebody walking up behind me. Oh, man, that's all I needed—to get carjacked and have to explain to my grandmother how I lost her car. I decided to just keep walking. When I got to the car, I turned.

"Hey, Kenisha, I thought that was you, what you doing around the way?"

Li'l T was standing there smiling like new money. "Hey, what's up, Li'l T," I said, too relieved to see him. "So what you doing around the way, girl?"

"I'm staying with my grandmother for a while. She lives near here."

"Nice," he said, "that means that your girl Chili will be hanging around, too, right?"

"I don't know about all that," I said.

"So where you going now?"

"I have to go to Freeman."

"Cool, why don't you give a brotha a ride?"

"You got a dance class?" I asked.

"Nah, I'm just hanging."

So we got in the car and I started driving. "Hey, why don't you take the shortcut?"

"What shortcut?"

"Turn right at the stop sign," he said. I turned and started following his directions.

"Is that the high school?" I asked, stopped at the light.

"Yeah, that's Penn Hall," he said.

Seeing Penn didn't impress me. It was huge and looked more like a prison than a high school. There were some guys playing basketball on the court across the street. The light changed. As I continued through I saw lawn mower guy. He was sweating and holding a basketball under his arm, so I presumed that he had just been on the court, but now he was just standing on the corner talking with a few other guys. He obviously recognized my grandmother's car 'cause he started staring real hard.

"Hey, do you know him?" I asked Li'l T.

"Who?" he asked, looking around all obvious. I seriously have to remember to school him on subtlety.

"That guy over there on the corner in the gray sweats holding the basketball talking to those other guys."

"Who, him, yeah, I know him, why?"

"I'm just asking, what's his name?"

"I thought you were seeing that wannabe NBA basketball player. He be 'round the way always talking trash about going to the NBA. Ain't nobody hearing that."

"I am, I'm just asking 'cause I've seen him around."

"Yeah, yeah, whatever, that was what I'm talking about, y'all girls always go after those bad-boy player types. A brotha like me ain't got a chance."

"Bad-boy types, what do you mean?"

"You know, bad boys like the movie, back in the day he used to be in all kinds of trouble all the time." Then he started laughing. "Yo, I remember them saying that once he even...nah, nah, wait a minute, no freebies."

"What?"

"A'ight, check it out, I'll tell you what, let's make a deal. You hook me up with your girl Chili and I'll return the favor. Anything you want to know about him, all the juicy dirt and gossip."

"What, boy, please, I just asked if you knew his name. I don't want to get all dramatic."

"Yeah, sure, they all say that about...uh...nah, no freebies." He started laughing again. "You get me in with Chili and I'll hook you up, digits and all. Turn right at this stop sign."

"Okay, as for Chili, you need to chill out with all that. She's not your type, trust me, and for your information, I'm not trying to get hooked up, I just asked a simple question, that's all."

"Uh-huh, they all say that about him."

"I should kick your little tired blackmailing butt out the car."

"Go ahead, 'cause we're here, hah," he said, then started laughing as if he'd just pulled off the greatest prank in the world.

He was right, we were right in front of Freeman. So I pulled into the small parking lot next door and we got out. Li'l T immediately ran across the street after seeing one of his friends. I went on inside.

"Hey, Ms. Jay, how you doing?" I called out, seeing Ms. Jamison, the dance school manager, locking the award and trophy cabinet. Ms. Jay was supposed to have been a serious dancer in her day but broke something in her back or cracked something or hurt something and had to quit her dream permanently.

"Hi, Kenisha, what are you doing here this early? Your class isn't usually until late this afternoon."

"I'm looking for my cousin, Jade."

"Oh, Jade's upstairs in the back studio."

"Thanks," I said, then walked down the hall against the wall seeing the newer students practicing tap, clicking their toes and heels. I smiled, remembering when I was young and having to practice the same wash step for what seemed like hours.

So as I went upstairs and I heard a serious beat going down. I checked the first three studios and saw that they were empty, then I went to the last one and stood at the glass window and saw Jade's reflection in the mirror inside dancing.

Wow.

I just stood there staring 'cause I couldn't believe what I was seeing. Her dancing was too tight. She was all over the floor and she was seriously kicking it out. The beat was heavy and her body was popping and jerking like she was a pro. When the music stopped, I heard thunderous clapping and realized that it was me. Jade turned around and stared at me for a minute like she had no idea who I was, then she turned back and nodded and smiled at someone else.

I opened the door and walked inside and saw Gayle Harmon standing in front of the mirror on the side, nodding her head. "That was hot, but it might be too tricky to pull off on the second downbeat. Let's try it again but this time try something like this." She did this body movement, turned, then paused to jerk back.

"Okay," Jade said as Gayle walked back to turn on the music again.

"You want something?" Jade asked, looking in my direction.

She walked to the side, picked up a bottle of water, drank, then picked up a towel and dried her moist face, arms and chest. At first I didn't say anything, I just stood there like a complete fool. Apparently I was getting good at this looking-like-a-fool thing. Then I coughed slightly like I had something in my throat. "Yeah, I mean yes, Grandmom wanted to know what time you'd be in this afternoon. She needs us to do something for her, I think."

"Umm—" Jade looked at Gayle "—umm, maybe around one or two o'clock."

I nodded and turned to leave.

"Wait," Gayle said. I stopped in my tracks. "Do you dance? Does she dance?" she asked Jade.

I turned around and saw Jade nod, still slightly breathless from dancing. "Yeah," Jade said.

"Why don't you show her the steps and see if it's too tricky on the second downbeat like we thought."

"I don't have my dance shoes with me," I said.

"Don't worry about it, your sneaks are fine, come on."

I walked over as Gayle reset the music.

"Gayle, this is Kenisha Lewis," Jade said.

"Hi," I said, then walked over to shake Gayle's hand, praying that my hand wasn't all sweaty. "I'm Jade's cousin."

"Oh, I didn't know you had a cousin in dance, too."

"Come on, Kenisha, let me show you the first few steps of the routine."

I swear I was on cloud nine for the next three hours. Dancing with Jade was really cool, then when Gayle joined in we were seriously burning up the wood. After a while Jade and Gayle just started changing moves and doing choreography and I just did the steps. It was like straight off the street raw, bump the clubs and the synchronized dance studios, their steps were way hotter than that stuff.

By the time we finished, Gayle had a routine that was too hot. I found out that it was for a video for Tyrece's new release that no one had even heard of yet. They, I mean Gayle and Jade, talked about the video concept. I was surprised at how tight Jade, Gayle and Tyrece were.

Afterwards we sat against the back wall, drinking water and talking about our favorite dancers. Needless to say, the list was long.

"I'm starved," Jade said, stretching her legs out.

"Me, too, what's your grandmother got going on?" Gayle asked.

They both looked at me like I should know. I shrugged, then it hit me, I did know. "Oh, right. She's making seafood gumbo."

"For real?" Gayle asked. I nodded, hoping that was really what she was making for today and not for some other time.

Jade and Gayle started laughing, so of course I looked at them, totally missing the joke. "Tyrece loves Grandmom's gumbo and he's gonna miss it," Jade said, filling me in on the joke.

"Tyrece, like in T.G., like in Tyrece Grant, he knows Grandmom?"

"She doesn't know?" Gayle said to Jade. Jade shook her head. Gayle nodded and smiled. "Oh, we were all just over to the house after we wrapped the video last week. She fixed this huge spread and we seriously threw down like there was no tomorrow."

It was my turn to laugh. "I can't believe it, everybody was all waiting down at the pizza place for y'all to show up. Somebody said that Tyrece was gonna be there, so just about everybody showed up to see him."

"That was why we didn't go," Gayle and Jade said, joining in with my laughter.

We eventually packed the CD player and stuff up and got ready to go. So as we're leaving, Diamond and Jalisa were standing in the front hall. I said hi and introduced them to Gayle. They already knew Jade. Of course they were speechless and pissed that they'd missed out on dancing with Gayle.

"We wondered what happened to you," Jalisa said. "Diamond and I were just going to try and go to your grandmother's house, but we couldn't remember exactly where it was."

"Well, come on," I said, "I have her car."

Diamond drove with Jalisa, following me, Gayle and Jade in my grandmother's car. We pulled up in front and we all got out. Lawn mower guy was there talking to my grandmom.

"Hey," he said, hugging Gayle and Jade, then he smiled at me as we headed down the path to the front porch. He grabbed the packages I carried and winked sneakily, like we had some kind of secret or something. I could see Jalisa and Diamond out of the corner of my eye looking at me and smiling. I knew I was gonna have some explaining to do later on, but thankfully he left right after he put the bags in the kitchen.

So we all went inside and ate and laughed and talked

about dance and videos and music. Then Jade took Gayle back to Freeman and Diamond took Jalisa back to Virginia.

As soon as I finished helping my grandmother clean up the kitchen, my cell rang, it was Diamond, and then Jalisa came on, too. I went to my bedroom so I could talk, and my grandmother headed off to something happening at her church.

"You heifer, you, you were dancing with Gayle Harmon upstairs and didn't even bother to let your girls know. I can't believe you even did that," Diamond said.

"Tell her," Jalisa said, adding to the teasing.

"It was too hot, they are too much," I said. "I still can't believe it. We listened to Tyrece's newest remixed single that was not even out to the radio stations yet and it was hot. Then we worked on outlining his next video."

"OMG, girl, I am so jealous," Jalisa said jokingly.

"Me, too," Diamond added. We laughed 'cause I just knew that both of them were too happy for me.

"Wait a minute, wait a minute," Jalisa said, stopping our laughter, "what I want to know is who is the cutie with the dimples and does he have a brother..."

"...or cousin, or best friend, or half brother, or next-door neighbor..." Diamond continued.

"He just hangs around. I don't even know his name."

"Get out of here."

"How can you not know his name?"

"We've never really been introduced."

"What do you call him, then?"

"Lawn mower guy," I said truthfully.

We all broke up laughing, then I heard the door slam and I heard my mom calling my name. I told Diamond and Jalisa that I'd call them back and I hung up. As soon as I did, I heard my mom scream for me at the top of her lungs. I went running downstairs to see what was up. We met in the second-floor hallway.

"What the hell did you tell your father?"

"What, nothing, why?"

"I just came from my attorney's office and he said that your father is cutting me off completely and that he's making arrangements to take you from me. I'm apparently an unfit mother now."

My mouth dropped open. "I didn't say that, I didn't say anything to him at all about you."

"Well, your father's attorney seems to think you did, so he's got me going to court to prove that I'm fit."

"Mom…"

"Call your father now and tell him…"

"Why don't you call him?" I asked.

"You call him now," she said.

"I'm not calling him."

"You need to stop being so damn selfish," she said.

"Me, selfish? What about you? You spend all day and half the night asleep or drugged-out because of those stupid pills you take. That's all you ever do, that's all you ever did, take pills and pretend that everything was all right. Appearances matter, right? You're a hypocrite, doping yourself up so you don't have to bother with life, with me, remember me? Your daughter."

"I knew you were angry and pissed off when you left

out of here Sunday evening, but I never thought you would go behind my back and…"

"I didn't, I didn't say anything like that."

"Kenisha…"

"Mom…"

"I don't want to hear it. I did all this for you, to give you a home, a better life, advantages that I didn't have. I sacrificed everything for you, and this is how you thank me, by being selfish and spoiled and going behind my back?" she screamed.

"What, what did you do for me? You made me leave my house, my friends, my school, everything, and come here. I didn't ask for this, I didn't even have a choice!" I yelled back. "I hate this place, I hate you."

"I can't believe how selfish you are. Everything is always about you, what you want, what's good for you. What about the rest of the world? Grow up, Kenisha, the world don't revolve around you or what you want. Sometimes we have to do what's best for someone else. I damn near cut her out of my life to make it better for you and you're gonna stand there whining about what you want and what you don't want. I wanted something, too. I wanted a life, but I made a choice, I committed to it and I lived with it for fifteen years."

"Is that supposed to be my drama? If you didn't want me, you should have just aborted me or gave me away. I didn't ask to be here. I didn't ask you to make a choice. You did it, now you live with it."

The slap came hard and loud. My left eye blurred and the side of my face felt like it had exploded. "You want to go back there and live with them, fine, go, I don't care anymore, go."

I didn't wait around after that. I ran down the steps and straight out the front door, barefoot, shorts and a T-shirt, hair wild to the wind, no money, no nothing. I had no idea what I was doing or where I was going, I just started running.

I guess I was about eight blocks away when I slowed down and stopped, and then it was only because I couldn't breathe anymore. My chest was on fire and about to burst. I started coughing and sputtering as I tried to get gasps of air into my lungs.

"Hey," I barely heard somebody, a male, say as he came up behind me, "you okay?"

I think I tried to say something, but only a gasping, raspy sound came out. I held on to my chest as my legs weakened and I stumbled, but somebody caught me, so I leaned on, trying to get my balance again.

"You're asthmatic?" he asked through my fog. I nodded weakly. "Do you have an inhaler with you?" I shook my head. "Okay, I'm gonna get you back home. Can you walk?" I shook my head again, hoping I could, but I guess I couldn't—'cause I almost collapsed when I tried. "Okay, why don't we sit down here a minute. You need to take a break before we walk back."

I had no idea what was happening or who was talking to me, all I knew was that I was running back home, to my real home in Virginia, where everything was perfect, where my life was perfect.

So I sat there, somewhere, with my hair all over my face, half crying and half gasping and looking like some crazy derelict or nut job from the loony bin. I coughed and wheezed and my head was spinning, I guess half from the slap and half from the asthma, and I was trying to focus on who was talking to me, but I had no idea.

I heard this person talking and his voice sounded kind of familiar, but my head was too hazy, it could have been Marvin the Martian from a Bugs Bunny cartoon and I wouldn't have known the difference. I think he was talking on a cell or something, telling somebody to come get us.

Now all of a sudden I got scared. What was I thinking? I tried to stand up, but my legs wobbled and crumbled beneath me and my head was spinning and my lungs were almost gone. A few minutes later, I guess, 'cause I really didn't know, I saw these headlights coming, flashing bright toward me and then I really got scared. I heard brakes screech and the only thing I could think of was that this person was going to take me someplace, rape and kill me, and nobody would ever know what happened.

So I reached up and scratched the mess out of his face. I'd seen enough *CSI* television shows to know that if I was gonna get killed, I was taking a piece of this asshole with me. Somebody grabbed my hands and I felt somebody pick me up.

Fine, whatever, my life was over.

CHAPTER 13

A Short Goodbye

"As if I don't have enough drama in my life right now, I still keep wondering when the other shoe is gonna drop. My mind floods with images of losing control, I just want to let go."

—myspace.com

LATER. The side of my face was throbbing and my head was spinning all over the place. I heard talking.

"...you need to stop taking all those pills and talk to that child. She needs to know..."

"...how am I supposed to tell her that everything she knows is a lie?"

"...tell her."

The next thing I remember I was lying in my bed and my mom was sitting beside me with a cold ice pack on the side of my face. Jade was a blur sitting at the window and my grandmother was leaning behind my mom, looking down at me. "Kenisha. Kenisha, wake up, are you okay?"

I took a deep breath and realized that I could actually breathe again. "I...just...need...to...catch...my...breath," I said, slowly and haltingly.

My head was still spinning, but things were clearer than before.

"Here, open your mouth and take this."

"No," I said when I saw my mom holding the inhaler up for me. "No more, I'm fine."

"Is she okay?" I heard Jade ask.

I nodded as my mother answered.

"She'll be fine, sweetie, don't worry," my mom said.

"It's good to have you back, baby. Come on, Jade, let's give her some room. You make us some herbal tea and I'll get some cookies," my grandmother said before she left and I saw Jade follow her out.

"I'm sorry, baby," my mom said, holding my hand tight.

"No, I'm sorry, but Mom seriously, I'm not lying. I didn't say anything like that to Dad. It was probably that skank Courtney."

"You know about Courtney?"

"Dad had her there at the house on Sunday."

"I thought you were going to meet him at a restaurant."

"I wanted to see the house again. I thought I could talk to him and make everything the way it was. Maybe you two could get back together and everything would be right again."

"Honey, everything is right again. You're back here with me and Jade and Momma, and my family is back the way it should be. The way it should have been. I should have never broken it apart. How's your face feel?"

"It still stings. I gotta learn how you do that," I joked.

She half smiled, but I could see that she was still concerned. "It's all in the flat of the hand and in the wrist action." We laughed, strange, but we did. She shook her head as tears began to fall. "I'm sorry for hurting you, and I guess I've hurt you more than I can even realize."

I shook my head. "No, Mom you're hurting yourself."

"When did you get so smart?" she asked, still half smiling.

A moment of placid calm passed between us and for the first time in a long time, it felt good to be with her, the real her.

"So you're getting a divorce, right?" I said. She shook her head and looked me straight in the eye. "What, you're not getting a divorce? What about alimony, don't we need that?"

"We don't need to get a divorce. Your father and I never got married."

"What?" I sat up too quickly. Big mistake, my head started spinning again.

"Baby." She sighed heavily and looked away, then back at me, holding the cold pack to my face again. "He always promised that we'd get married and I always meant to push him, but I never did. After you were born I just never did. Then time just slipped away for both of us."

"You're not married to Dad?" I repeated, trying to wrap my head around what she had just told me. "That's why he could just up and make us leave like squatters or something, the restraining order." She didn't say anything, so I knew it was true. "Okay, so what now, palimony?" I asked her.

"Your father's attorney talked to my attorney."

"And?"

"He said he'd pay two hundred dollars a month in child support and that was it. He told me to sell the furniture and jewelry I took if I needed more cash and that if I wanted you to have more, I'd have to give you up, since I was unfit to care for you anyway."

"He said that?"

"His attorney was far kinder."

"Okay, what about school, Hazelhurst, will he pay for that?"

"No, he said it would be good for you to go to a D.C. public school for a while, to gain perspective."

My mouth dropped open. I couldn't believe it, he made all those promises and he lied and I knew Courtney had something to do with it, too.

"Kenisha, I can't get unemployment benefits—I haven't worked in over fifteen years. Your father has completely cut me off. This is our home now. Mamma isn't rich, but she's a port in the storm. We've had our differences and I'm trying to make amends. But baby, this is our life now."

I nodded. "I know." The dizzying feeling returned and I didn't want to talk about it anymore.

"Does grandmom know?"

"Yes."

"About you and Dad not being married, I mean."

"Yes."

"That was what the two of you were fighting about before, when you stopped speaking, wasn't it?"

"I thought that we didn't need a piece of paper to be committed to each other." She half smiled at the memory. "We decided that our love would hold us strong, bond us together forever, till death us do part," she said. "I was wrong."

"Mom, is that why you and Grandmom stopped speaking?" I asked again, thinking she didn't hear me the first time.

"No, no, it wasn't," she said, then looked directly at me.

Even though I suspected she was lying, the truth in her eyes was so sincere, I believed her. "And Jade, does she know?"

"Yes, she knows, too."

I nodded my head. "Everybody knew but me."

"Not everybody, just us."

"That's everybody," I whispered and lay back.

"I know, I failed you, I failed Jade and I failed myself, but you two are the only good things in my life," she said in a strong, determined voice.

"I'm tired, Mom."

"Sure baby, lie back, get some rest, everything will be better in the morning. I love you, always remember that."

"Me, too," I said.

When she left, I started wondering about what she had said about making amends and about failing and about her life. All those years, she was waiting for something more to happen to her and never stepped up to do it herself. Then for some reason, I remembered what my grandmom had said to me about making a decision, committing to it, then learning to live with it. I guess that was what my mom did. I guess that's what I have to do.

I guess I fell asleep, 'cause I kind of woke up a while

later. It was late. I got up and went to the bathroom. Jade's door was cracked open and I heard my mom in there talking to her. I went over and listened.

"Jade, you are an incredible young woman, far better than I was at your age. You're smart, in control and focused. You're a role model, you have goals and purpose, with a determination that I could only dream about. Your future is endless."

"So is yours. So what if James let you go, that was his stupidity. You have so much going for you. You can do anything you want."

"No, it's too late for me, I'm through."

"You're just barely over thirty. It's not too late, you can do anything, go back to school. I'll even take a computer engineering class with you."

"I did so many stupid things, all in the name of love, first with you and then Kenisha. Don't follow my example and don't let Kenisha. I know the two of you aren't close right now, but help her to understand," she said.

"I don't want to talk about that."

"Yes, we should, we need to. She was a child, she didn't know any better. It was my fault, I should have protected you, I should have stepped up and said something. But I was so afraid of losing everything, and look, I lost everything anyway. Because of me, your life..."

"No, don't even think that, because of you I had, no, I *have* a wonderful life. I'm happy, really happy, school is great, I dance, I have my friends, I have Grandmom, you and Kenisha, and I have T."

"Are you still seeing him even after everything?"

"Yes," Jade said, "but we don't exactly broadcast it."

"Obviously, not even to me."

"You knew about him before."

"I didn't know you were still together. Just be careful, baby. Don't lose yourself, don't ever lose yourself."

I inched closer, wondering who they were talking about, and hoped to hear a name. 'Cause after living with her for over a week, I never even saw Jade talk to a guy, let alone hang out.

"Do you love him?" my mom asked her.

"Yes," Jade said.

"Does he make you happy?"

"Very."

"Jade..."

"I know what you're gonna say. But I'm an excellent student, and not just with books and school, with life. I'm not saying that I have all the answers, I don't, but I do have Grandmom's recipes."

I heard them laughing, so I stepped back a little.

"Your father would have been so proud of you, the way you are, the way you turned out."

"I miss him so much. Sometimes I can't remember what he even looked like," Jade said.

"Do you still have the locket I gave you?"

"Yes, here."

I stepped back more, then went back to my bedroom, wondering about their conversation. It was odd. I didn't know that my mom was so close to her niece. She must have been really close to Hannah Mae, too. Then I started feeling a little jealous. I didn't remember us ever having talks like that. She was just always getting on my case about stuff.

A little while later, my mom came to my room and was standing there in the doorway like she wanted to say something, but she didn't. She just stood there and I realized that my life was so busy with nothing that I hadn't actually spoken to her in the few days before our argument tonight. She stayed locked up in her room most of the time, taking her pills and being depressed. She didn't say anything for a while, she just stood there.

I looked up at her as if to say, what? She still didn't speak. So I looked at her again, hard this time, and seeing her now, I saw that she wasn't the same woman. Earlier, she was a screaming banshee, all pale and wild, ready to kick my ass. But all that was gone.

The first thing I noticed was that she looked different, all tired and beat down. Her eyes were red and blood-shot. I don't know how or when, but I know that there was something else different about her. She looked like she had drowned and this shell standing there was all that was left of her.

See, my mom was perfect, nails, hair, makeup, clothes, jewelry, she was always tight and on top of her game. She put on some weight from time to time, but all she did then was take her diet pills and she was right back to perfection within a couple of months.

But looking at her now, you wouldn't know it. I'm not sure when it happened, when my mom changed into this person standing here now, this person I don't even recognize. She was hurting, dealing with her own drama and fighting her own demons. I guess maybe I was too busy all this time, locked up in my own drama to notice hers.

I wonder if she'd cried out for help, and if I wasn't there or just wasn't listening. I looked at her and started hurting for her. Not for me, for her.

"I love you, Kenisha, I always will, know that."

"I know, and I love you. Mom, do you still love Dad?"

She paused a moment and stared at me, then finally answered. "No. Does that upset you?"

I shook my head. For some reason, it didn't. "Did you ever?"

"There was a time, a long time ago." She half smiled. "A lifetime ago."

She walked away silently, back downstairs to her bedroom, back to the tiny white pills that helped her sleep. They took her pain away and she let them, although tonight was different, tonight they took everything.

Ambulance.

Police.

Rescue team.

Hospital.

Doctors.

Morgue.

My mom died at 3:32 in the morning.

CHAPTER 14

Back Home Again

"When did I become the ultimate narcissist, selfish, self-centered, self-seeking, addicted to me. When did I start living in my own hermetically sealed, self-important world? When did it all revolve around me?"

—*myspace.com*

I SWEAR I'm too young to feel this old.

Death, I looked it up on the Internet: shock, denial, bargaining, guilt, anger, depression and acceptance, the seven stages of grief. Where did they get this stuff? I wasn't feeling none of that. I was just feeling empty inside.

It was the next day or the day after that. I got kind of confused, so I really don't remember. All I know is that the house was quiet at first, 'cause basically everybody stopped talking to everybody else. We all just walked around like lifeless shadows cast against a wall, all dark and blurred, out of focus, bumping into solids but not really being there. It was obvious that they blamed me. That was okay 'cause I blamed me, too.

I killed my mother and seeing them meant facing my guilt. So I avoided them. It seemed a lot easier 'cause I didn't feel like dealing with all that. I was the reason she couldn't sleep, I was the reason she took the pills, I was the reason she got mad that night and I was the reason she died, plain and simple.

So all I wanted now was solitude.

My grandmother's next-door neighbor and best friend, Mrs. Harrison, came over. She said that we were all still in shock; but all I knew was that I didn't cry and I wanted to 'cause everybody else seemed to be. So what was wrong with me? Why couldn't I feel anything?

No. I did feel something, I felt cold. It was near ninety degrees out and I was cold. A chill went through me and stopped and I felt like I had fallen into a frozen slime-coated pit with no way out. I couldn't eat or sleep or anything. So I just stayed in my bedroom, sweater on, bundled up, alone, hoping nobody would figure out that it was me.

'Cause bottom line, somebody died and it was a fact that somebody had to be blamed. We argued big-time that night, and she got really pissed at me. Maybe that was the catalyst that spiked it all and started the whole thing. Maybe that was why I couldn't cry, 'cause I knew it was all my fault.

Like a flash fire in dried kindling, word about my mom got around fast, 'cause all of a sudden all these people started coming over to the house. Things got confusing, but my grandmother's church ladies, who arrived early

every morning and left late every night, came by and basically took over everything.

Every other minute the phone or doorbell would ring
and somebody else wanted into my world. They either
came or called; my friends, too, but I couldn't deal with
them, either. I didn't want to talk to anybody. I was still
trying to make sense out of it all. I knew what the police
had said and what the detectives and the doctors and the
coroner had said about it being nobody's fault, but I just
wasn't hearing none of that.

My grandmother sat in the living room mostly. That was
where people came to see her. I didn't know where Jade was.
She left yesterday morning and I haven't seen her since.

So I sat there in my bedroom, cold and waiting in the
bottom of my open slime-covered pit. Then there was a
knock on the door. "Who is it?"

"It's me, Diamond."

"Diamond?"

"Yeah, can I come in?"

"Yeah, sure, come in," I said, turning from the window.
Diamond came in quietly and walked over and stood at
the window seat beside me. "How'd you find out?" I asked
her.

"You know my grandmother and your grandmother go
to the same church." I nodded, realizing that her grandmother was probably one of the church ladies that always
came by. "I told Jalisa, I hope that was okay." I nodded
again. "Can I do anything?" she asked.

"No." I turned back to the window.

"I know you probably don't feel like talking and that's

okay, I just wanted to stop by and say hi and see how you were doing. My mom's downstairs, she said to say hi, too." I nodded. "Your grandmother told me to bring these up." She set a small tray of cookies on the table beside me. "She said that if you want something to drink that you had to go downstairs and get it, but I snuck this up for you." She pulled a Diet Pepsi out of her hoodie jacket pocket.

"Thanks," I said, smiling for the first time in a long time. "I'm not really thirsty."

She put the soda beside the cookies and sat down next to me. She looked out and saw the backyard and the treetop view. "Nice view, you can almost see Virginia from here."

"Yeah, almost."

"When's the funeral?"

"Day after tomorrow."

"I'll be there. I'm going with my mom and grand-mother," she said, picking up a cookie and breaking it in half, handing one half to me.

"Thanks," I said, then took a bite of the cookie.

So we sat there nibbling cookies for a while and looking out the window. "I killed my mom," I heard myself confess to her. I looked up and saw her look at me. I expected her to be shocked or pissed or hurt, but she wasn't. She was just sitting there looking at me. "I killed my mom," I repeated.

"No, you didn't," she said. "My grandmother said it was her heart."

"No, we had an argument and she slapped me and I ran off. I couldn't breathe and..."

"Kenisha, listen to me," she said, sliding closer, "you and your mom argued all the time. Please, girl, me and my mom argue all the time, too, you know that, that didn't mean anything. It's just words. We get pissed, they get pissed, so what? They get it. Just 'cause you two fought doesn't mean anything. If that was the case, every teenager in the world would be in jail for murder and there'd be nobody left."

"But it was a real bad argument."

"Yeah, so," she said, brushing me off. "Listen, you didn't kill your mom, and that's it, hear me?"

"Then why can't I cry?"

"What?"

"Why can't I cry for her, everybody else is crying."

"Maybe it hasn't hit you yet. Not everybody feels loss or pain at the same time. I remember when my grandfather died a few years ago, it took me a long time to cry and to get my feelings out. I was still in shock 'cause I loved him so much. You know I never knew my dad 'cause he died overseas in the marines, so my grandfather was like everything to me. He even took me out on my first date, remember," she said.

I nodded and smiled, remembering our Girl Scouts father and daughter date we all went on years ago. My dad took me, Diamond's grandfather took her and Jalisa's older brother, Brian, took her 'cause her dad was overseas.

"So, trust me, when the time is right, you'll cry, okay, okay?" she said again. I nodded. "Good, so guess what," she said, seeming to want to change the subject and lighten my mood, "your lawn mower guy is downstairs."

"Who?"

She nodded, chewing the chocolate chip cookie. "You know who, your lawn mower guy is downstairs. He asked me to tell you hi," she said. I guess I looked skeptical 'cause she smiled. "He did, I swear. I think he seriously likes you."

"First of all he's not my lawn mower guy."

"Yeah, right," she said, popping the soda cap and taking a short sip, then handing it to me.

"For real," I said after sipping the soda then handing it back to her. "He's always around hanging out with my grandmother and walking in and out of here like he pays rent or something."

"'Cause he likes you," she repeated, smiling wide, "and you like him, don't you?"

"Hardly, no," I said haughtily, rolling my eyes and pushing my nose as high up in the air as possible. "Besides, I don't even know his name."

"Please, as if that really makes a difference, so what, unless of course it's something stupid, like maybe Herman, or Jasper or Percival or Urkel." She laughed. I looked at her and shook my head, half smiling. Diamond had a way of making people smile. "No, wait, how about Vlad or Frank N. Stein."

I chuckled. "You are so silly," I said.

After that, talking got easier, then joking and laughter followed. After a while I was back. I climbed out of the slime-covered pit and I was back. Then somebody knocked on my door again. "Come in," I said, hearing my voice sound a lot better.

Jalisa came in, followed by Chili.

"Hey, how you doing, girl?" Jalisa said, walking over to me and Diamond. But before I could answer, Chili started acting up.

"What's that bitch doing here?"

"Chili…" Jalisa started.

"No, what's up with the skank being all up in here. I thought we were through with her."

"This is not the time for your drama," Jalisa said.

Diamond reached over and took my hand and squeezed it. "I gotta go anyway. My grandmother's probably downstairs making everybody crazy and my mom's probably ready to go. You take care. Call me if you need me."

"Thanks for coming," I said.

"That's right, step your ass out of here, skank," Chili hissed.

"Chili, you need to stop, you know you can be such a jerk sometimes, what is your problem?" Jalisa asked as she hurried to follow Diamond out.

"What, who me? I ain't do nothing." She grabbed a cookie and started eating it. "Y'all always up in my face with that, blaming me for something. You need to talk about her, she the one all up in here knowing can't nobody stand her ass." When the door closed, Chili looked at me and smiled. "Hey, girl, so what's up, and who is that fine-ass brotha downstairs, his dimples are hot and he's got those light-colored eyes, damn, his babies with me would be gorgeous."

Chili always sized up a guy by what she thought their

children would look like. "You know, he was seriously checking my shit out. I think I might just break a piece off of his fine ass." As per Chili, every guy on the planet between the ages of ten and fifty wanted to get with her.

Okay, so then I looked at her like she had lost her mind, and she wasn't even paying attention. She was so far in Chili-world that she had no idea that her stuff was messed up. When did the world start revolving around Chili Rodriguez? So then I wondered if I was blind to everything around me just like her.

"No, you didn't just come in here with that," I said.

"What?"

"Acting all stupid like that," I added.

"What are you talking about?"

"This is my house and my room, don't be throwing people out of here."

"I thought you didn't like her."

"We started talking again, we're cool."

"No accounting for taste," she said, sucking her teeth.

"Whatever," I said, but at that point, Chili had gone way past getting on my nerves.

"Don't think I'm supposed to like her now, 'cause I don't."

"I didn't ask you to."

"Good, so when you moving back to Virginia?"

"I don't know."

"What, I thought that this was what you wanted; everything can be like it was before now, right?"

"No, my mom's dead, everything can't be like it was before."

"I know she's dead, but what I mean is that you can

move back into the house with your dad like you wanted to before."

"I don't know, maybe, I don't know."

"What do you mean you don't know, what's wrong with you? Hello, look around, Kenisha, this place is whacked. I don't know how you even live here. It's all dark and ugly and old. No disrespect to you grandmother and all, but damn, this place is hideous. The only good thing is that brotha downstairs."

"Why do you do that?"

"Do what?"

"Trash everything and act like every man on this planet wants your tired, no-English-speaking ass."

"'Cause they do," she said arrogantly, striking a pose.

"No, they don't, they just want what you can do for them."

"So, at least I do it," she snapped.

"What's that supposed to mean?" I asked her.

"Nothing, forget it."

"Oh, I see you been talking to LaVon. Well, he's right. I'm not giving it up to him and nobody else until I feel like it."

"That's your problem, Kenisha, it's all about you."

"Look who's talking, thinking you so hot that every guy on the planet wants you."

"That's right, they all do."

"I don't think so."

"Your man do."

"*Did*, past tense, that was from that grammar class you skipped last semester."

"Do, he still do want me," she said awkwardly.

I didn't know why I wasn't shocked. "Well, then, you can have him," I said, then we just stopped and started staring and gritting on each other.

"You are a trip," Jalisa said as soon as she came back in. "Can't you act like you have sense sometimes?"

"Ain't nothing wrong with me, what's wrong with y'all, all hugged up with Diamond and all like she somebody. That skank tried to step up on my shit and take my boyfriend. Look, y'all acting all stupid and I'm tired of all this drama. I'm going, if you want to get a ride back to Virginia, come on, 'cause I'm leaving now." The words came out fast and confusing.

"What did you say?" Jalisa asked.

"Don't start that shit with me, Jalisa, you heard me."

"I'm staying," Jalisa said, smiling.

Chili slammed out and we looked at each other and burst out laughing. "That girl needs to have 'drama queen' tattooed to her ass as a federal warning label," I said.

"She's a trip," Jalisa agreed, "and her whole future-trophy-wife-drama thing is seriously getting tired, real fast."

"Tell me about it. Is Diamond okay, I mean, after Chili and all?"

"Yeah, she's fine. I'm gonna meet her at Freeman later. But I'm glad the two of you are okay now."

I nodded. "Yeah, me, too."

"You think Diamond and Chili will ever get back?"

"Knowing Chili, I doubt it. She's still too pissed and embarrassed. But you know Diamond was wrong acting like that at Chili's sweet sixteen party. She should have just walked away instead of dealing with that drama.

Getting caught kissing Chili's boyfriend at her own party was too wrong."

"She said that fool grabbed and started kissing all over her and that he wouldn't let her go."

"I can see that, you know he had a thing for her and the only reason he started with Chili was 'cause he couldn't get Diamond, but still, she should have known Chili was gonna blame her for her boyfriend's stupidity."

"I'm telling you, Chili is getting crazy." I nodded. "But I'm glad Diamond stopped by. She said that she's going to the, you know, funeral, so I'm gonna catch a ride with her and her mom and grandmom. My mom and Nat are coming, too, but I'm gonna stay at Diamond's house, so…" I nodded again. She picked up a cookie, broke it in half and handed one half to me. I took it and smiled. It was good to have my girls back. "I saw your new boyfriend downstairs."

"What new boyfriend?" I asked, knowing exactly who she was talking about.

"You know who I'm talkin' about. He was downstairs and I swear he was waiting for you to come down."

So just as we started talking, my grandmother called me downstairs. "There's a young man down here who would like a word with you," she said when I got to the top of the stairs.

I looked at Jalisa. Both of us were thinking the same thing, lawn mower guy. I could feel my face starting to get warm. "Go get your new man, girl," Jalisa said.

When we got to the top of the landing, I saw lawn mower guy standing in the foyer getting ready to leave. I had to admit, it was really good to see him. I started smiling, and he smiled back and nodded his head. I got to the bottom of the stairs, then I felt Jalisa pluck me in my back and I stopped and turned around. She opened her eyes wide in warning, but I was totally confused.

"Okay, Kenisha, I'm gonna meet Diamond at Freeman. I'll catch up with you later. Call me." Then she looked behind me. "Hey, LaVon, how you doing."

I turned around just in time to see lawn mower guy walk out the front door and LaVon come out of the living room toward me.

"Bye," I said, glad Jalisa had stopped me from walking over to lawn mower guy with LaVon standing right there.

"Hey, shorty," he said, then walked over to me, completely oblivious of my almost mess-up. "I was gonna call you, but I decided to just stop by."

"Hey," I said, closing my eyes and folding myself into his arms and trying to remember all the good times we'd shared. When I opened my eyes, I saw that other people were looking at us. So I suggested that we step outside.

"How she die?" LaVon asked as soon as I sat down on the front step beside him. Then a couple of women came up the front path.

"You must be Barbra Jean's daughter, you look just like her, bless her soul. How you doing, baby? I'm Mrs. Coles. I knew you mommy when she was just a baby, too. I'm so sorry to hear about her passing, she was a blessing."

I smiled and nodded. "Thank you."

"Where are Jade and your grandmother?"

"Grandmom's inside. I think Jade is still out."

"Well, let me go say my piece with them. I brought a dish of sweet potato soufflé with marshmallows, pecans and honey. Come in and get a plate, it'll put some meat on you."

"I will, I promise. See you later."

She continued past us after a brief nod to LaVon.

We scooted back together, then someone came out and gave me a hug and told me to be brave. When they left, we moved together again.

"I guess it hasn't hit me yet that my mom's really gone. I kinda don't remember stuff."

"How she die?" LaVon asked again.

"They have to do more tests, but they said that it might be an aortic aneurysm."

"What's an aortic aneurysm?"

"Um, it's basically when a part of the aorta, the main blood vessel close to the heart, swells up. The bulge got so big that it eventually ruptured, she hemorrhaged, dying almost immediately. They said that the buildup of pills in her system might have helped weaken the blood vessel. It's rare, but some people are affected like that."

"Damn, that's messed up," he said.

"Yeah, it is."

"So what are you gonna do now, live with your dad?"

"I don't know, maybe, probably."

"Good, you should come back to Virginia."

"You think so?"

"Yeah, I miss you."

I looked into his eyes and felt his sincerity. It felt good hearing him say that, but just when I was about to say something, somebody walked by, so we scooted over to let them pass.

"Come on, let's go upstairs and talk in private."

As soon as I walked back inside, I saw Jade talking to one of the women who had just walked in. She nodded her head and I returned the greeting.

LaVon and I went upstairs, but didn't talk long. As soon as we got to my bedroom, we started kissing and then touching and I could feel him getting all excited as usual. So I started pushing him off. "Okay, LaVon, stop." But he kept kissing me and feeling all over me. I panicked. "Come on, stop, I can't."

"Aw, come on, not this shit again. Come on, Kenisha, your mom is gone, we can do it now," he said.

"What you think, it was my mom that was stopping me before?"

"Yeah, I know she didn't like me, so fine, she's out of the picture. We can do it now." He reached out to me and I swatted his hand away.

"Do you realize that my mom just *died*?"

"Yeah."

"And there's a house full of people downstairs, including my grandmother and cousin?"

"Yeah."

"And you don't care?"

"I'm trying to make you feel better," he professed.

"LaVon, you gotta go."

"Shit, I'm tired of this on-and-off-again with you. You're just a tease and I'm tired of it, do you know I got girls lined up around the corner to get with me? I don't even know why I bother with you. I guess I just felt sorry you." He stood up and stomped over to the door. "Don't come looking for me when I blow up, begging for this, 'cause you lost out. The NBA is hard on me and you could have gotten a free ride."

"You know what, LaVon, I don't want a free ride. I don't need a man to cash my check. I might just meet your ass at the NBA as an owner and fire your butt."

"You know, you can be such a bitch sometimes," he said.

"That's right, and proud of it," I said.

"I'm out of here. You call me when you're ready to step up and be a woman." He walked out, leaving the door open. I heard him going downstairs. I could tell he was still pissed. But I really didn't care.

I wanted to lash out. I wanted to cry. I wanted to scream and yell and throw things. I wanted to cry. But really I just wanted to feel something, anything. Two days and I'm a blank. Why couldn't I cry?

CHAPTER 15

Too Damn Bad

*"When your back's up against the wall and you don't
know which way to turn, you lash out and anyone who
gets in the way, for them, well, that's just too damn bad."*
—*myspace.com*

I stared at the open door for a while and even considered going back downstairs to catch up with LaVon,
but I knew I didn't want to deal with all that. So I decided
instead to slip out the back door and just leave. I went
out into the hall, then heard a typing noise coming from
Jade's bedroom. The door was slightly ajar, so I peeked
inside. She was sitting at her computer desk with her back
to me. I opened the door more. "Hey," I said, peeking
farther in.

She turned around. "Hey."

"Are you busy?"

"Just instant-messaging a friend," she said, signing off,
"but they have to go anyway."

"May I come in?"

"Yeah, come on in," she said as she logged off, got up and sat down on her bed while I went over and stood by the front window, looking out. I saw a car pull up and several people get out and walk toward the house.

"There are a lot of people downstairs. I didn't know Mom had so many friends."

"Everybody liked her."

"I know you and my mom were close…" I started, but realized that I didn't know what to say to finish the conversation. "I mean, she talked to you a lot, right?"

She looked up at me. "Yeah, I guess we do. Did."

"I don't know what to do anymore," I heard myself confess to her. "It's like I want to go to her and talk to her and ask her what to do, but I can't and I'm lost."

"I know, I am, too," she said.

"I miss her."

She nodded. "Yeah, I miss her, too." Then she started crying, tears just started falling nonstop. I went over to her and wrapped my arms around her and together we sat there. She cried and I held on, wishing I could.

"So I guess we finally have something in common. Both our moms died young and unmarried."

"She told you," Jade said after grabbing a tissue and wiping her eyes dry.

"Yeah, she told me the night she died. I can't believe that all this time I didn't know, but I guess it doesn't matter now that she's gone."

"What do you mean?" she said.

"Since my mom and dad never got married, she didn't

have anything in her name. Not the house, not the cars, nothing. I guess I probably have to go back to live with my dad, but he's got his pregnant girlfriend living up in the house and now all my friends are gonna know."

"Is that all you care about, where you gonna live and what your friends are gonna know?" she said, standing up. "I can't believe you. I am so sick of your whining about what you want and what you don't have. Oh, poor Kenisha, life is so hard for her. Do you think you're the only one in pain here, the only one hurting? You're not. I hurt, too."

"But she was my mother. Her death changes my life."

"Oh, so you hurt more?"

"I didn't say that, it's just different, that's all. We had a bond, a mother-daughter bond. She was only your aunt."

"My aunt," she said, shaking her head. "You still don't have a clue, do you? You're still the spoiled little brat only thinking of yourself. You just said that she told you."

"She did."

"Obviously not everything."

"What are you talking about, not everything?"

"Get out."

"No, what do you mean, I want to know."

"Fine, *I'll* leave."

She brushed past me, so I grabbed her arm.

"Oh, you think you can take me?"

"What is wrong with you? You've been on my case since I got here and even before then. Did I do something to you as a kid, call you a name, cut your doll's hair, spit in your Kool-Aid or something? Whatever it was, you need to get over it."

"You need to get out of my face, Kenisha."

"Or what?" I asked, too tired of her crap.

"Or I'm gonna beat you down, hard."

"You think you bad, try it, go ahead!" I screamed back at her. She screamed at me and we went at it full force until our grandmother came busting in.

"Stop it, stop it, stop it, both of you, you hear me? Stop it! What's wrong with you two, screaming and yelling like you have no sense? This house is in mourning. My daughter is dead, your mother is dead, have some respect for her memory."

"It wasn't me, it was her. I don't know what your problem is, Jade, but you seriously need to get some professional help," I said, ready to get started again.

"Forget you," Jade said, snapping back fiercely.

"All right now, that's enough, I've had it, both of you. Jade, get over there. Kenisha, you move over there. I don't want to hear another word from either one of you," she said as she looked at each of us.

"You girls listen to me. My daughter loved both of you, fiercely, completely, unconditionally, without reservation. She did everything in her power to keep you safe. So much so that it broke her heart to separate you. She tore herself apart trying to do the right thing for each of you. So I don't want to hear this fighting when her body isn't even in the ground yet."

"If you weren't so blind to everything that doesn't center around you, you would have known..." Jade sniped.

"Hush up, Jade. Now, both of you listen to me, families are born, not made. And yes, I know you have your friends that are your family, too. But blood is different. You two share my daughter's heart, now act like it."

Jade walked out.

I was about to walk out, too, but my grandmother stopped me. "Kenisha, come back here and sit down," she said. I didn't. "I said sit," she insisted. I sat down.

"We have a funeral to attend tomorrow, and I'm not gonna disgrace my daughter's memory with this bickering. Do you understand me?"

I nodded.

She wrapped her arms around me then took my hand and held on tight. "Oh, baby, I know this is unfair to you, as much as it was unfair to Jade all those years ago, lost. It was wrong to keep this from you, but it was your mother's wish. She was going to tell you in her time, but time ran out on her."

"I know, she told me."

"Now that this is out in the open, you need to talk to Jade. Grief has struck her just as hard as you, maybe even more. She didn't have her mother around all the time, like you did. She feels like she lost a mother twice, once to you and now to death. You both need each other now more than ever."

"Why didn't Mom tell me before? I don't get it, it's really no big deal."

"What exactly did your mother tell you?"

"She knew I'd be upset and I was, but really, I don't care that her and Dad weren't married all this time."

"Oh, Lord, she didn't tell you."

CHAPTER 16

Enough

"I remember this song before, about saying goodbye, I don't remember who sang it or the lyrics or when or where I heard it, I just remember this song before, about saying goodbye."

—*myspace.com*

I didn't remember sleeping, but I must have 'cause I woke up cold again. I remember the day being bright and sunny and hot, but I was still freezing. I had goose bumps and chills all morning and I couldn't get warm. It was Saturday, the day of my mom's funeral. It was sad. That's all I have to say about that.

So later I was sitting there at the grave site next to my family, next to Jade, and we were both just staring ahead, looking at the casket as it was going down into the ground. I felt empty and I guess Jade was feeling it, too. I reached over and took her hand, I didn't know why, I guess I just needed so badly to touch something real, someone who was a part of my mom. But her hand was limp, wilted and dead, just like my mom's as she lay there with her eyes closed, locked in her forever place.

Mostly everybody was there. I talked to Jalisa and Diamond and Chili at the funeral, but LaVon was a no-show. I wasn't surprised. He was weird about stuff like that.

So when it was over and the preacher said his words, we stood up and dropped a long-stemmed rose from Grandmom's garden on the casket into the ground. Mine landed right next to Jade's. I guess Mom had finally brought us together. 'Cause after that, we didn't move, we just stood there, both of us looking down.

Everybody else started leaving. Then I saw my dad. He shook a few hands and hugged some people, making his way through the leaving crowd toward me. He looked old, tired and broken.

"Hi, baby girl," he said.

"Hi, Dad," I choked out.

He stood a minute looking down at Mom's casket. "You must really hate me," he said, standing there beside me and Jade and my mom.

I was just about to answer as Jade turned to walk away. But my dad turned to her. "Jade," he called out. She stopped and turned, then looked at him as if he were a small child. "I know you must really hate me," he said.

"Why would I hate you?" Jade asked in that way she did that made a person feel like they were two inches tall.

"For what I did to you all those years ago. I was wrong. I realize that I should have handled it differently, but I didn't and I can't change what happened, but I want to do the right thing now. I want you to come live with Kenisha at the house. You'll have your own room, your own things."

"I have my own room, my own things," she said.

"You know what I mean, I can give you things, things your grandmother can't, money, an education, a life, a family, a future."

"There's nothing you can give me that I don't already have, James." She tilted her head and looked at him with pity then walked away.

I stood there in silence like it was someone else's life I was witnessing, 'cause I still didn't feel anything.

My dad put his arm around me and I just stood there looking down into the hole. The dark wood, mahogany, and brass looked speckled as a light drizzle started.

"Kenisha," my grandmother said, "are you ready?"

"She's coming home with me," my dad answered.

"Kenisha." She touched my arm. I turned. "Come on, child, it's time to go home."

"She's coming home with me," my dad said again.

I looked at my grandmother. She stood there in quiet indignation. "I'm sorry, Grandmom."

She nodded and half smiled. "Remember your recipes," she whispered, then turned and walked away.

Her words echoed in my head. "The recipe to make your own history is to decide what you want, commit to your decision, then be able to live with the consequences. Follow your heart. It'll never let you down."

I turned back to my mother and said goodbye one last time.

"Come on, baby girl, let's go."

I followed him to his car and got in. I sat there looking at the sea of tombstones as my dad drove out of the cemetery. We were heading home and I realized that I still didn't get it.

"Mom told me that you two never got married," I said as he drove. He didn't answer. "Did you hear me, you never married Mom?"

"No, we didn't feel the need for a piece of paper."

"All these years and you never said anything?"

"You were too young."

"I'm fifteen."

"You were young at the time. It would have been confusing, it was better to leave things as they were."

"Better for who? It's the twenty-first century, not 1952. If you weren't married, fine. But why didn't you tell me? And what about all those anniversaries?"

"Okay, fine, maybe it was a mistake not to tell you. I was trying to protect you."

"Protect me from what?"

"Gossip."

"I repeat, it's the twenty-first century."

"My family was broken up by gossip."

"There are a lot of couples that choose not to marry, so that's not even the issue. Did you ever love her?"

"Yes, I loved your mother very much, too much."

"What's that supposed to mean?" I asked. He didn't say anything. "Okay then, what about Courtney, if you loved Mom so much or as you said, too much, why did you do her?"

"I didn't *do* her, get that straight," he said, changing his tone. "What Courtney and I have is different. The business isn't doing well, and Courtney was there for me when your mother wasn't. She was always too busy."

"So you love her, too, right?"

"Yes."

"But you can't have two wives, two families, so you tossed the old one out."

"No, it wasn't like that. It's complicated."

I didn't say anything after that. I didn't see the need. So that was it for that conversation. We pulled up to my grandmother's house for me to grab some clothes and a few things. A few minutes later, I walked out with two suitcases.

As soon as we got to my old house, as soon as I walked in, I felt the bitterness rise up in my throat. The cheap stench of Courtney was all over the place. And I started to wonder what I was doing there.

"Welcome home, dear," Courtney said, her teeth gritted painfully as she smiled openly at my dad. Her pregnant belly protruding, she was dressed in a full-length black sequined gown, with her flawless makeup and sparkling paste jewelry, she looked at me victoriously as I just stared at her in disbelief.

"Kenisha, I want this to work, I want us all to be a family. Do you think you can do this?" my father said to me, but before I could reply—

"Daddy, Daddy, where's my toy. You said that you were gonna bring me a toy when you got back, where's my toy?"

"My toy, too, Daddy," another boy echoed, following the first. They ran up to my father and grabbed at his legs.

I just stood there, my mouth wide open. "Did they just call you Daddy?"

"Junior, Jason." He reached down and picked up both small boys, holding each protectively in his arms and smiling as if the sun rose and set in their eyes. "There's my boys, hey, buddies, I want you to meet somebody." He looked at me and smiled weakly.

"Kenisha, these are you baby brothers, James T. Lewis Junior, and Jason Mitchell Lewis. Hey, buddies, can you say hi to your big sister?"

"No, I want my toy, you promised," the older one said.

"You promised," the younger one repeated.

My dad smiled weakly again. "Now, come on, be big boys. I told you that I was gonna to bring you a surprise, and here she is, Kenisha. Can you say 'Kenisha'?"

"No," the older one insisted, then wiggled free until his feet touched the floor, then he ran to Courtney. "I want my toy, I want my toy. Mom…" The other followed exactly, both now holding on to Courtney with her protruding belly.

"I want my toy, I want my toy," they chanted over and over again. I just looked at the four of them, stunned into disbelief. Where was I when my father was starting a family all over again?

"Don't touch me," Courtney said, holding the boys away from her at arm's length. "James, I told you to bring them something, now how are we gonna be on time with them screaming like this? Come on and get dressed, I don't want to be later than we already are."

My dad looked at me. "Kenisha, Courtney and I were wondering if you'd look after Junior and Jason for us. We have a formal dinner to attend and since you're old enough to babysit, we thought this would be a way for you and our sons, your brothers, to get to know each other. Uh, I'll pay you, of course."

The words kept tumbling out of his mouth, one right after the other in a succession of words with meanings that were completely foreign to me. I just stared at him as he turned and hurried upstairs.

"Look, Kenisha," Courtney said, "we've had our differences and I'm sorry about your mother, but your dad and I are in love, and we have been for a while. It was only a matter of time before this ended anyway. He never wanted you to leave. It was your mother that insisted you leave with her. And since you had wanted to stay here, it's all set."

She reached down and straightened one of the little boys' T-shirts and tied the other one's sneaker. "So in the end everyone got exactly what they wanted, right? No harm done. You can babysit Junior and Jason from now on while we go out, and when our daughter is born, you can…"

"My mother's dead," I heard myself saying.

"What?" she asked, looking up at me after tying the sneaker.

"Everybody didn't get what they wanted. My mother's dead," I clarified.

"You didn't like her anyway, right?"

Okay, I had a choice, slap her or walk away. Open palm, all in the wrist. At that moment I was my mother's child. I slapped the hell out of the heifer and almost broke my watch in the process.

She screamed, the two little boys took off, yelling, and my dad came running down the steps at top speed.

"Courtney, Kenisha, what the hell happened?"

"Your skanky little bitch hit me!" Courtney screamed, holding the side of her face as it turned bloodred and as her eye started to swell and a trickle of blood came from her nose and lip.

I was so proud of myself, and I knew that my mom would have been proud of me, too.

"Kenisha, what the hell is wrong with you? Go to your room!" he ordered, like that would mean something to me.

I smiled and winked at Courtney and sashayed my ass to the front stairs with my suitcases. I heard her scream at my dad and I started to chuckle.

"That was it, go to your room? Is that all you're gonna do? That bitch hit me in the face and you send her to her room? What's wrong with you, kick her ass out."

"Courtney, she's my daughter and I need to—"

"I don't give a shit what she is, what you need to do is kick her little ass, and you better not just let her walk away with that or I'll…" she threatened.

I was midway up the stairs when I heard her threaten him. I stopped and smiled, waiting to hear her ultimatum.

Typical Courtney, she had nothing.

"Fine, whatever, you just better make damn sure that that hellion of yours keeps her damn hands to herself. If she puts her hand on me again I'm gonna kick her ass, pregnant or not."

"Don't upset yourself. Why don't you get an ice pack and a cold glass of water and calm down, I'll handle this."

By that time I was upstairs, but I could hear every word they said. I went to my old bedroom. It was empty, same as the last time I saw it. I smiled some satisfaction for my mother. If Courtney thought I was a hellion now, she ain't seen nothing yet.

"Kenisha," my dad said, knocking on my open door and coming in. I sat on the bare wood window seat, looking out. I didn't turn when he came in and I didn't answer him. "Kenisha, I know this is very difficult for you. And we will talk about this when I get back. If you could just babysit Junior and Jason tonight, I promise you I will..."

"Will what?" I turned to him.

"Kenisha, just babysit the boys, that's all I ask."

"Do you really think that's gonna happen?" I asked him fiercely.

I guess the snide smile on my face and the look in my eyes made him nervous, 'cause he got right up and went downstairs to talk to Courtney.

"...maybe this isn't the right time..."

"...oh, hell, no, I'm not changing my plans..."

"...her mother just died, this is too much to ask..."

"What, but it's our anniversary!" I heard her scream. "Why the hell do we have to miss it because of her drama? You're her father, make her babysit."

"Do you really want that?"

I heard my dad's low mumble, then more of Courtney's shrieks of annoyance. I smiled. Same old, same old. It was a small victory but it felt good to screw up his drama for a change. Payback was going to seriously be a bitch named Kenisha.

CHAPTER 17

A New Home Again

"How do you drown out reality when it's falling down all around you? I guess you don't. Drama comes down too hard, like boulders down a vertical landslide. You can't rewind, you can't fast forward, so you just push pause and wait for the end."

—*myspace.com*

It had been five days since the funeral, almost a week. I was back at my old house, but it didn't feel like home anymore, my mom wasn't there, my real things weren't there, so it wasn't home for me. Out of necessity my dad pushed this tired, lumpy old bed into my room and expected that it was good enough. He was wrong. But I guess it showed me my new place around here.

Every day was pretty much the same. I stayed in my room mostly, then sometimes when I did get dragged downstairs, it was to eat or to hear my dad lecture me about depression while Courtney rolled her eyes and sulked and complained about my attitude and what I didn't do around there.

What exactly did they expect?

As far as I was concerned I was doing okay, considering. It still didn't seem real and my heart was ripped knowing that I'd never see or talk to my mom again, but I knew that it was time to get my life back together, so last night I called LaVon for the first time since before the funeral. As usual he didn't pick up, so I left a message, then two minutes later he called me back.

"Hey, I was just thinking about you," he said, as if the last seven days hadn't happened and everything was all right.

"Hi," I said, hearing my voice still low and monotone.

"Are you back now?" he asked.

"Back from where?" I asked him.

"D.C."

"Yeah, for the time being, I guess, why?"

"Good 'cause I'm not about to be driving my car down there in that neighborhood anymore."

"What's wrong with the neighborhood?"

"Like you don't know, the place is shit. I ain't gonna front, that hood is whacked. One of my boys told me that this guy around there stabbed this other guy, then shot him like seven times, then went after dude's whole family just because he wanted his ride."

"That doesn't even sound right," I said.

"Yo, I'm just saying…"

"That's so lame, it's not even worth being called an urban myth."

"Whatever, but those hoodrats play for real and I ain't about to be getting all mixed up in that. My ride is too sweet and I don't want to have to blow my scholarship for some mess like that. The place is whacked and the people are whacked, the end."

I didn't say anything at first 'cause I realized that that was me a few weeks ago. He continued complaining about no place to park his precious car and the thugs hanging out scoping on him and his ride, but it was going in one ear and out the other 'cause I just wasn't listening. I realized that whatever he was talking about just didn't matter. "It's not that bad," I finally said in defense.

"What, you drugging in the hood now, girl?" he joked. "Taking those pills."

That hit too close to the heart. "Why do you have to tear everything down?" I asked.

"It was a joke, yo, can't you take a joke anymore?" he said, getting all defensive. Then for a few minutes we both went silent, but he was still there, 'cause I could hear a sportscaster on television in the background.

"What, you don't feel like talking now?" I asked him.

"I don't know, maybe later," he said.

"Why don't you come over and hang out?" I offered.

"Nah, I gotta take care of some business," he said, giving me the now standard answer.

"A'ight, later." I hung up.

Yeah, I knew things between us were getting bad again and usually I tried to do something about it, but the truth was I just didn't care. A few minutes later I called my friends, finally returning their dozen or so calls from the past five days. Jalisa was at work, Diamond was at Freeman and Chili was just someplace else.

Anyway, I didn't sleep again that night, but then I didn't really expect to. I stayed up thinking mostly, about my mom and about my dad. I was still finding it hard to believe that nobody stepped up on that and told me the truth. But what was done was done. So now I was thinking, what else didn't I know? There had to be more to all that.

My dad had two kids and one on the way, somebody had to have known about that. If my mom knew, she didn't tell me. So it didn't make sense that my mom, who'd always preached about doing the right thing, living up to my potential and looking out for my future, would just decide that she didn't want to be married. Yeah, there had to have been more.

So now considering everything, I didn't think my grandmother was gonna say much more, since her only advice was always that I needed to talk to Jade. So I thought maybe I'd take her advice. That is, if she'd talk to me.

I knew what I had to do, I just wasn't sure I was up to it, so I stayed in bed and finally fell asleep just before dawn. I woke up with the usual empty feeling. Every day I seemed to feel guiltier.

I got up around ten, showered, got dressed and tried calling Jalisa, but she wasn't around again, neither was Diamond. I didn't know what the problem was, since at the funeral they were like serious milk carton missing.

So I went downstairs and saw Courtney sitting in the living room folding laundry with her two boys at her feet crashing toy trucks on my mom's once flawlessly polished hardwood floor. My mother was probably turning in her grave.

"It's about time you got up, Kenisha, I have some things I need you do this morning," Courtney said, setting the laundry basket aside.

"Where's my dad?" I asked her.

"He's not here."

"Where is he?" I asked more directly.

"He's at work, busy, so don't disturb him like you usually do with one of your childish tantrums," she said. "Now sit down, we need to talk."

"I have to go," I said, figuring I would stop at my dad's office before heading out to talk to Jade.

"Where do you think you're going?"

"Out."

"No, not today, you have things to do around here."

"Really," I said, then turned around and stood there, waiting for her to say something. But of course I knew she was gonna give me the whole "I'm the HNIC" speech, so why not, I was up for a little comic relief this morning.

"Yes, really, and don't give me that attitude. First of all, I need to get some furniture in here..."

Oh, no, she wasn't gonna tell me to move my mother's stuff back in there.

"...and your father wants me to get the stuff out of storage, so I need to know the name of the company your mother used when she moved everything out," she said. Meanwhile one of her kids started hitting her leg and calling her over and over again.

"Mom, Mom, Mom, Mom..."

I looked at her like she'd lost her mind. If she and my dad thought that it was gonna be that easy, then they had another thing coming. "I don't remember," I said, giving her my innocent expression that had never worked with my mom, then I turned around to leave.

"Wait a minute," she said, standing and taking a step toward me. I stopped and turned around again, very obviously annoyed. "You were there, weren't you?"

"Mom, Mom, Mom, Mom…" the youngest chanted.

"Where?" I asked.

"Where, here, you were here when the truck moved everything out," she said, clearly getting exasperated.

"Oh," I said, "uh, no, I mean, yeah, sometimes."

"What is that supposed to mean?" she asked.

"Mom, Mom, Mom, Mom…"

"I mean, I was here, then I left then I came back."

"So what was the name of the company?"

I looked up at the ceiling, then shook my head and smiled. "I don't remember."

"Mom, Mom, Mom, Mom…" he continued.

"Kenisha," she said through gritting teeth, "I'm sick and tired of putting up with your princess candy-ass attitude around here…"

"Ohhh, you said a bad word, princess candy-ass…"

"…your father's not here, it's just you and me, and I'm tired of playing with you. I'm marrying your father and if you intend to keep living here, you'd better get one thing straight. I run this house now, not you."

"Princess candy-ass, princess-candy ass…" the oldest started chanting.

Here comes the HNIC speech, I thought. I smiled innocently and waited. And to think I actually liked her at first.

"Mom, Mom, Mom, Mom..." the youngest whined.

"You ran your mother into the grave, but don't you even think about trying that shit with me. I'm not having it," she said, and meanwhile, her youngest son, who'd been calling her all along, was now crying and screaming his head off as the oldest kept chanting, then rolling and hitting him on the leg with a toy truck.

"Stop it, stop it, y'all shut up, you stop hitting him and you wipe your nose and stop crying," she yelled to them.

I looked at her, then down at the two kids and shook my head. She was in way over her head. "Is that all?" I asked.

"No. You have chores to do this morning. I need you to clean the bathrooms upstairs and wash the kitchen floor. Then do something with the pool. Your father said that you usually take care of it anyway, so do the chemicals and clean it out. The boys want to go swimming this afternoon and it's a mess."

"Yeah, swimming, swimming, swimming..." The two boys immediately started singing and jumping up and down behind her. They dug into her already folded clothes in the basket and pulled out shorts, then started stripping down. I smiled, knowing that she didn't need me to give her grief, she had my father's sons.

"Also your father and I are going out tonight, so you need to be here to babysit." I smiled, knowing that none of that was going to happen, and she seemed to read my mind. I turned around and headed out, hearing her call after me. "I'm not playing with you, Kenisha, and I'm not putting up with your crap."

I just kept walking. The last thing I saw were the two little boys dancing and jumping around stark naked.

"Swimming, swimming, swimming, swimming, swimming…" they sang, and began running around butt-naked.

"What the hell, pick those clothes up, stop it, get back here and put your clothes back on, I'm not playing with you…"

I almost felt sorry for her, but then again the more I thought about it, the more angry I got. Courtney actually thought that I was just gonna fork over everything just because my mom wasn't around anymore. No way. And my dad was seriously losing his mind if that was what he thought, too.

So now instead of catching the Metro train to my grandmother's house, I took the local bus into northwest D.C. My dad's office was in the heart of the business district, in one of those super-exclusive high-rise office buildings. It had been a few months since I'd been there and it looked different, but I guess it was the same. It just seemed different, or maybe it was just me.

As soon as I walked into his office, some of the people I knew came over and hugged me and gave their condolences and sympathies. The receptionist, Mrs. Taylor, said that my dad was on the phone, so I sat and talked to her while I waited. Well, actually, she talked.

"I remember Barbra when she first came here," Mrs. Taylor started, like she always did with her "I remember when" stories.

"You do?" I said obligatorily, knowing that Mrs. Taylor, being the oldest person in the office, insisted on acting like everybody's mom or grandmom. She was nice and all, and I even remember her baking cookies every Christmas when I was a kid and having them on the desk when Mom brought me in to visit.

"Lord, she was a skinny little thing back then. Of course she was just a teenager then, just a little older than you, tiny thing, so happy, but boy did she know computers, she could fix any computer in a matter of minutes, understood them real well, even taught me a trick or two. She was still in school then, was engaged to be married."

"Married?" I asked, suddenly interested. "To my dad?"

"Oh, no, some other young man in school with her, I believe. Working here was her freshman internship and he—" she paused "—now, what was that boy's name…"

How do you just drop a story to try and remember a name from over fifteen years ago? So I waited while she was still thinking. "Don't worry about the name, Mrs. Taylor," I said, "don't worry, it doesn't matter."

"It'll come to me, probably while I'm cooking dinner tonight. Anyways, he would stop by from time to time to pick your mother up after work. Nice young man, very mannerly, but when you mother saw you father, it was all over. I could tell right then she was already smitten, and your father was smitten with her, too."

The conversation went on from there as Mrs. Taylor started talking about the company they used now for computer problems and how inefficient they were.

That was okay, since I was only half listening anyway.

Then my dad's office door opened and this young woman I didn't recognize walked out. They shook hands and she smiled that smile and I knew right then that he was on the move. He glanced around the office quickly as he pivoted to go back inside, then I guess he saw me stand up, 'cause he did a double-take as I walked over.

"Kenisha, what are you doing here?" he asked with a chill of stunned civility then he looked at Mrs. Taylor and smiled, welcoming me with open arms for appearance's sake.

I played along, then walked into his office and sat down as he followed and sat behind his desk. "I don't suppose the rest of the office knows about Courtney moving in," I said.

"As a matter of fact, they do," he said, but I could tell he was lying. "I'm glad you stopped by, did Courtney talk to you about the furniture?"

"What furniture?" I asked. He just looked at me hard. I guess Courtney had already called him about our little conversation. "Oh, yeah, that, I don't remember."

"That's what she said." I shrugged. "The storage bill is going to have to be paid eventually, so holding out isn't going to get the money." I shrugged again. "Kenisha…"

"If Courtney wants furniture, buy her some," I said.

"That's not the point and you know it," he said. I shrugged again.

"All right, I've been trying to be patient with you because of the situation, but my patience is about to wear thin. You hitting Courtney was unacceptable, and you will listen to her and to me and do as we say. And if I want you to babysit the boys, then that's what you're going to do, do you understand me? You're under my roof and there are rules."

"Are you going to marry her?"

"What?"

"Are you going to marry Courtney?"

"I don't know."

"She seems to think so."

"That's not the topic of discussion at the moment."

At that point I realized for the first time that I had no idea who this man was. I was just about to respond when his cell phone rang. He looked at the caller ID. I could tell it was Courtney, so I got up and walked out. I'm sure he didn't even know I was gone.

"Jaden, Jaden," Mrs. Taylor said as soon as I came out of the office. "His name was Jaden."

"Thanks, Mrs. Taylor, see you later."

As soon as I got outside I took a deep breath, filling my lungs with clean, fresh air. The stagnant stink of his trash-talking was stifling. I headed to my grandmother's house to talk to Jade.

CHAPTER 18

Unconnected-Connected

"I want to make it right, so I have to start at the beginning and unravel everything I think I knew, then somehow start knitting together a new vision of my life, drawing yarn from all around me."

—*myspace.com*

SO I got off the Metro and of course there were these guys hanging out on the corner. They weren't doing anything, just standing there laughing, joking and messing with anybody passing by. I wasn't in the mood to deal with their crap, so I decided to cross the street to avoid drama. Then don't you know, one of them crossed the street to walk directly toward me. Did I really need this drama now?

I don't think so.

"Hey, baby, how you doin'?" this one guy said as his friends started whooping and hollering and cheering him on. I just walked by him, ignoring him, refusing to break my stride. I must have been seriously moving 'cause the brotha had to hurry to catch up with me.

"Yo, shorty, wait up, let me holla at ya," he said, taking a long drag of his cigarette while tugging at the oversized jeans that hung at least six inches below his narrow hips. I don't know why guys think that looks hot, 'cause it don't.

Of course I didn't answer, I never did. I figured that if I didn't reply, he'd eventually get the hint, I was wrong.

"Whoa, baby, you are packin' some serious heat back there." I glanced across the street in an effort to ignore him. "A'ight, a'ight, I'm just messin' wit ya, you a'ight, for real. So what's up, where you going to?" I began to roll the image of me pushing this no-talking fool up underneath this bus coming down the street and started smiling to myself.

"Uh-huh, I see you grinning, a'ight, a'ight, that's cool, you ain't gotta talk, you're going my way, so mind if I walk with you, these streets can be dangerous sometimes," he said, adjusting the trifolded red and white scarf tied on his head so that the tied knot was poking through his left eyebrow.

So we started walking and he started talking and I wasn't paying any attention until he started talking about hanging out at the pizza place with Tyrece Grant and how the two of them were tight and all.

"Yo, yo, snaps, don't I know you from somewhere?"

"No," I finally snapped, still walking.

"Jada, right, that's your name, I remember, Jada something."

"No, my name isn't Jada anything."

"A'ight, a'ight," he said, seemingly breathless from the forced march and the cigarette hanging from his lips, "I gotta check you later, my cell's ringing." He slowed down, then I guess eventually stopped, because by the time I reached my grandmother's street, I was walking by myself.

Four houses away, I could see that there were people over, 'cause of all the parked cars on the corner. And nobody parked there unless they were going to her house. So since I wasn't ready to see my grandmother after I'd just left her like that at the cemetery, I decided to slip in the back door.

I opened the front gate and walked around to the side of the house, then got to the back steps. The screen door was open and I could hear voices, then I saw that several women were in the kitchen, including my grandmother. I stepped back to try and figure out what to do next. Then I heard somebody call out.

"Hey, shorty."

"Can't you take a hint, leave me alone," I snapped, turning around, expecting to see the guy with the scarf over his eye. But instead it was lawn mower guy. I didn't know why I felt relief in seeing him, but I did. Then I guess what I'd said hit him 'cause he backed away. "No, no, wait, not you, I thought you was some other guy. You know, somebody on the street."

He nodded. "Come on, this way," he said, motioning for me to follow him. I did.

We walked toward the shed in the backyard. Behind it was a gate leading out onto the small patch of land between my grandmother's house and the next street behind her. "Where are we going?" I asked, looking at the narrow walkway with a few young boys tossing a football.

"Come on," he said, opening the gate for me. I walked through, then stopped and waited for him to lead again. I followed him along the back fence to the house next door. He opened their gate and we walked into the yard, then over to the back steps and sat down.

"You didn't look like you were ready to go in there."

"I wasn't, thanks," I said.

"How you doing, you okay?" he asked. I shrugged noncommittally. "Never mind, dumb question," he added, then paused as we watched a butterfly flutter past then settle on a bright yellow flower. "I'm sorry about your mom. She was nice to talk to, I liked her."

"You didn't even know her," I smirked.

"Yeah, I did. She came around all the time."

"She did? Like, when?" I asked, looking at his profile as we sat side by side on the step.

"On the weekends mostly, in the afternoon, her and Jade would hang out in the yard or I'd see them out talking or shopping or something, or she'd be at Freeman."

That surprised me. Talking, shopping, hanging out. How was it that my mom visited Jade when I was hanging out with my friends and I knew nothing about it? I went quiet, thinking to myself and trying to figure out my mom and everything.

"Crying doesn't make you weak," he said.

"What?"

"I'm just saying, crying is okay."

"Yeah, I know, I get that."

"Being angry is okay, too."

"What are you, some kind of fortune-cookie dispenser?"

"And everybody feels pain in their own way, in their own time."

"Yeah, okay," I said, then watched the butterfly flutter away.

"I know you probably don't feel much like talking. I didn't, either, when my brother died."

"When was that?"

"It's weird, it was almost four years ago, but it seems like a lot longer. You know, it's funny, well, not funny, but strange. After he died I expected everything to be different, like the world was supposed to stop or something. But nothing changed, nothing happened, traffic kept moving and kids in the neighborhood were still outside playing. It was weird."

"I know, it is strange. It's like my mom died and nobody cared. And now I find out that she had a whole life that I knew nothing about. She had these dreams for me, my future, so now she's dead and I'm trying to figure out what I'm supposed to do now. It's not fair."

"No one ever said that life was fair," he said.

"Yeah, true, that," I said.

"Are you going to stay with your grandmother still?"

"I don't know," I heard myself say, "I don't know. I guess it's according to my dad. But I'm not about to deal with all that right now."

"Sometimes life just screws with you. You wake up one day and everything you think you know is just wrong."

I looked over at him. He was staring out across the yard

like he was seeing something that wasn't there. "So when did you get so profound?" I asked, being slightly sarcastic.

He smiled, cracking his dimple deep, then turned to look at me. "Are you kidding me, shorty? I'm a philosophical maven, seriously profound."

"Oh, really, that's not what I heard."

"What do you mean, what did you hear?"

"I heard about you. Whether it's true or not, I don't know, I'm just saying."

"So what did you hear?"

"That you're a bad-boy gangster player."

He laughed again, darting his dimple at me. "Nah, that must be someone else, not me."

"No, they said it was you, even pointed you out."

"All right, yeah, maybe I had a few things going on a while back. I had some drama, was even in the youth detention center for a while."

"A youth detention center, for what?" I asked.

He paused, then looked away. "I stabbed somebody."

"You stabbed somebody?" I asked as a chill went through my center. He nodded. All of the sudden the cute guy I was sitting with turned into this dangerous thug, and I wanted to move away. "Why?" I asked cautiously.

"He deserved it."

"So it was like some kind of street cred or something, or a gang initiation thing?"

"We can't all be rich saints like you, shorty."

"That's not fair," I said.

"I told you, life's not fair."

"Fine, I gotta go," I said, suddenly feeling uncomfortable.

"So what, now you leaving, right, I'm a thug, you scared 'cause I stabbed somebody and went to youth detention, I'm a degenerate, right? Doesn't matter how it went down."

"No, it doesn't, you tried to kill somebody, you just admitted it."

"Yeah, I did, so what, go." He stood up and started to walk away.

"Wait, I didn't mean it that way. I'm sorry, it's just that, I mean…"

"Yeah, I know your type."

"That's unfair."

"You prejudge me and then you say I'm unfair," he said.

"Point taken."

He didn't leave. He just stood there.

"Did they die?"

He looked back at me with sincerity in his eyes. "No, he's still around, last I heard he was doing some serious time someplace in upstate New York."

"So what was it, an accident?"

"No. I intended to do it."

I nodded acceptingly. "Okay, why?"

"It doesn't matter now."

"Yeah, it does, I want to know."

"He killed my little brother for seven dollars and fifty-three cents, so we fought and I tried to kill him," he said simply. I looked at him, but instead of being nervous or scared, I kinda understood his anger. "So you still scared of me now?" he asked, rubbing at some fresh scratches on his face.

"No."

"Good." So we sat back down for a few minutes in a comfortable silence.

"So what happened to your face, some girl scratch you, or you get in another fight?"

"Oh, you gonna act like you don't know, huh?"

"Know what?" I asked, having no idea what he talking about.

"You frontin' on me like that, huh?"

"Seriously, what?"

"You scratched me." Okay, I was about to go off, then he started laughing, so I figured he was joking. "You don't remember, do you?"

"Remember what? I didn't scratch you."

"You ran out the house that night and I followed you. Shorty, you can run, no lie, 'cause I was on track in high school, and I could barely catch up with you. So then I guess you were having asthma problems, so I called your grandmother's house and your mom came and got you. I was talking to you, telling you that your mom was coming, then you said something about *CSI,* then scratched me."

"No I didn't," I said emphatically, then I kinda vaguely remembered, so my mouth dropped open. "Oh, man, I did that for real? Ohhh, I'm sorry, my bad, I thought I was dreaming. I'm sorry. I didn't mean to...I thought..."

"Yeah, I know, dreaming."

"Sorry, is it bad, does it hurt?"

"Nah, I'm cool," he said, rubbing the scratches again.

"Good," I said, then started laughing.

"You're laughing? You're sadistic, aren't you?"

"No," I added, still grinning. "So do you go to Penn High now?"

"No."

"The detention center still?"

"No."

"So what high school do you go to, then?"

"I'm out of school."

"You dropped out?"

"Do I look like I dropped out?" he asked.

Before I could answer, we looked over 'cause we heard my grandmother's screen door close, but whoever it was only stepped out for a second, 'cause there was nobody there now.

"Um, I guess I better go now."

"Back to Virginia?" he asked.

"No, not yet, I gotta find Jade first."

"She might be at Freeman."

I got up and took a few steps, then stopped and turned to him. He stood up and walked over to me. We stood there looking at each other, kinda smiling. "Thanks, for everything, see ya," I said, then kinda waited around for... I don't know what.

He leaned down and kissed me gently. "Later."

I swear, his lips were so soft and gentle. It was like he barely touched me. Definitely nothing like LaVon, he was always trying to grab me and pull my shirt off.

So after we kissed, I backed up and walked through the gates and saw my grandmother standing on the porch. I looked up at her, knowing that she must have just seen me and lawn mower guy kiss. "Hi, Grandmom," I said.

"Hello, Kenisha, are you back?" she asked.

"I don't know yet." She nodded. "I'm looking for Jade."

"She's at..."

"Yeah, yes, I know, I'm going there now."

"Why don't you come inside and get something to eat first. You look dead on your feet."

"I'm fine."

"That wasn't a request, Kenisha, come on in here and eat something and clean yourself up. I'm not having my grandchild walking around looking like she's half-starved."

"Yes, ma'am."

I went inside expecting to see the place packed. Nobody was there except me and her. I sat down at the kitchen table and she pulled out all this food and started heating it up. Twenty-five minutes later, I ate almost everything, not realizing that I was that hungry.

"He's a nice young man," she said finally.

I knew who she was talking about, of course. "I'm not interested. My boyfriend is headed for the NBA. He's about to make a lot of money and..."

"Lord, you're just like your mother. But you need to learn from her mistakes."

"What mistakes?"

"Having money isn't having worth. Just because some people live in a big fancy home in a real nice neighborhood don't make them good people. They're just people with things. Worth comes from inside, from love. You need to love and accept yourself first and foremost."

"But everybody loves themselves, right?"

"No, some don't. Some people live their whole life searching for someone to love and someone to love them and never realize that it's right there inside of them."

"Do you think that was why Mom took the pills?"

"I don't know."

"She was sad, wasn't she?"

"Yes, for a long time, a very long time," she said, staring out across the room like there was somebody else there with us. "Family comes to family for healing, remember that."

I had no idea what she was talking about, but I nodded anyway. After that I went to my room, took a shower and changed clothes. I packed a small bag, then got ready to leave. My grandmother was sitting on the front porch when I stepped outside. "You gonna be okay?" I asked her.

"I'll be fine, go do what you have to do. You know where home is."

I nodded, then walked the four or five blocks to Freeman, and as soon as I walked up I saw Jade's car parked out front. I went inside looking around for her.

"Kenisha, is that you?"

"Hi, Ms. Jay," I said, stepping back to peek into her office. I really wasn't in the mood to deal with anyone, but whatever.

"Hi, Kenisha," she said, sitting at her desk, "I didn't expect to see you here today."

"Is Jade here?"

"She's upstairs in the back studio. Go on up."

"Thanks," I said quickly.

"Kenisha, baby, I'm real sorry to hear about your mother. She was a good woman, really nice."

I nodded. I still had no idea what I was supposed to say. I went up to the private studios on the top floor and found Jade. I expected her to be dancing or something, but she wasn't. She was in there just standing at the window, looking outside. I opened the door and went inside. She looked up.

"Whatever it is, I don't want to hear it," she said before I even opened my mouth.

"Jade, I didn't come here to argue or fight..."

"Good, then you can leave."

"I just want to talk."

"I'm not in the mood for what you want, Kenisha."

"I just want to talk."

"Just leave me alone."

"Jade..."

"Fine, then I'll leave, as usual."

She started walking by me, so I grabbed her arm again and she snatched away hard, nearly knocking me down. "Are we gonna do this again?"

"No, please, just talk to me, please."

"What, what do you want now? What do I have that you want? You have everything and still you want more. What is your problem?"

"Jade..."

"I told you I didn't want to talk, but of course it doesn't matter what I want, it never did, 'cause it's always all about you. I'm sick of it and I'm sick of you."

So of course I just stood there, saying nothing. Then I

finally found my voice and spoke. "I don't know what you're talking about. I never did anything to you. You're just hateful and mean."

"Me, hateful and mean. Look who's talking."

"You have something to say, Jade, just say it."

"Your spoiled ass took her away."

"I took who away?"

"My mother!" she yelled.

"How did I take your mother? Hannah Mae died when I was a kid, I don't even remember her."

"Hannah Mae wasn't my mother, Barbra was. Yeah, that's right, she was my mother, too, okay, got that?"

My mouth dropped and stayed open a long time, then the air around me started to leave and the room was getting hot. "What do you mean your mother, too, what are you talking about? Your mother was Hannah Mae."

"Hannah Mae was our aunt and she never had kids."

"She had you."

"What are you, completely stupid or something? Barbra was my mother, fool. She had me three years before she had you."

"How is that possible?"

"After hearing you and your boyfriend in your bedroom last time, I would think you could figure out how it was possible."

"That's not what I mean, how is it that I didn't know?"

"You knew, I don't know why you're frontin'," she said accusingly.

"I did not. How was I supposed to know something like that? Nobody ever said anything to me."

"You knew, then James told you different."

"My dad?"

"Yeah, you remember we played together before when we were kids? Mom would come over and get me at Grandmom's house and we'd all hang out together. Then you told your father that I got a stupid doll and you didn't and that was the end of everything."

"What?" I said, completely crestfallen.

"Don't act like you didn't know."

I wasn't acting, seriously, my mind was completely gone. I had no idea what she was talking about. "I didn't know, I swear, I don't remember."

"You're just like your father, a selfish, conceited liar. The world centers around you, and everybody does exactly what you want. You walk around here all day like you're some kind of princess, a diva or something. Talking about 'I wanna go home, I wanna go home,' whining like a spoiled brat, you couldn't even see that all this was killing her. She hated her life and you were just too blinded by your own selfishness to even notice."

After that, she left. I stayed.

I swear my head was spinning in circles, thinking about what Jade had just told me about my mom, our mom. Then I started thinking that maybe she'd just lost her mind or maybe she was just messing with me and lying. But something inside told me she was telling the truth.

So the first thing I did was call my grandmother but there was no answer. Then I tried calling my dad, but he wasn't in the office. I headed back to my grandmother's house and she was out in the garden.

"Grandmom." She looked up from her planting. "Is Jade my sister?"

"She told you?"

"Yes. It's true, then."

"Good, it's about time."

"How come I didn't know? Why didn't anybody tell me?"

"Your father insisted that your mother tell you that Jade was your cousin. Then he forbid her from having you two together."

"Why? It doesn't make any sense."

"That, you're gonna have to ask him. But for right now, you need to settle this with Jade."

"How? She hates me."

"She doesn't hate you. She's hurt, that's all."

"Same thing," I said.

"She's family, she's your sister."

"As if it wasn't hard enough before, what am I supposed to do now, about Jade, about my dad? I know I can't be mad at her when she's dead."

"Yes, you can, you can be very mad."

"So how do you do it, how do you feel better? I don't understand, Grandmom, why did she have to die? I keep thinking that if I was better, stopped complaining, then maybe she would still be alive. I killed her."

"No, stop. Stop it right there. There is no blame and no guilt here. My baby died the way God planned. Nothing could have changed that. She was in our lives for a while, but it was her time to go."

"I didn't know it was the last time I would talk to her. I don't even remember what we talked about. I keep trying to remember, but I can't. I was so mad at her, but now I don't really remember why. But I know it was my fault she died. If we hadn't argued."

"Is that what you think, that it was your fault?"

"I know it was."

"No, baby, none of this is your fault."

"I gotta go," I said, then started walking.

"Where are you going?"

"Home."

I got half a block away, then stopped. So how was I supposed to face Jade? No wonder she hated my guts. My dad ruined her life, I ruined her life.

That was it, enough of this.

CHAPTER 19

Betrayal

"Trust is a hell of a thing to lose and once it's been betrayed, getting it back is close to impossible. Yeah, I fronted on people, I shoveled my bullshit, but stepping over the line is just plain wrong."

—*myspace.com*

"Damn, Kenisha, what, what's wrong now?" LaVon asked.

"Nothing, I'm fine, I want to do this, really. But I'm just…" I shrugged and looked up into his eyes and wondered what was behind them, love? "Umm, I'm just nervous."

"I'll take care of you, always, you know that. It's you and me, right, just like we planned," he said soothingly.

"Do you love me, LaVon, I mean, really love me?"

"You know I do, shorty," he said, but the sentiment never seemed to reach his eyes. They glowed strong with hunger and want and desire and affection, but not with love.

"And all those other girls…" I began.

"What other girls?" he asked, kissing my neck.

"The ones you kept talking about, the ones that are lined up around the corner wanting you."

"I was joking, you're the only one for me, you know that. I would never betray you, Kenisha, never."

I smiled as I saw the earnestness in his eyes. "That was all I wanted to hear." We kissed and it was for real. It was nice and I started to forget all that other stuff. I was safe and loved and nobody, no little white pills, no Courtney, no nothing, was gonna take this away from me.

"Relax, remember, I'll take care of everything."

"Do you have condoms?"

"We don't need them. It's your first time."

"Do you have condoms, LaVon?"

"Yeah, I got 'em, relax, okay."

"Yeah, okay. But can you get me a glass of water before we do it?" I asked, leaning away from him.

He rolled his eyes to the ceiling. "And that's it, right, we gonna do this, right?" I nodded. "A'ight, wait here, I'll be right back." He got up off the bed and grabbed his shirt up. As soon as he pulled it over his head, his phone rang.

"You gonna get that?" I asked.

"Nah, let it ring. I never pick up when I about to get busy."

The phone kept ringing and LaVon walked out. After a couple more rings the machine picked up. "Yo, this is LaVon, holler."

"LaVon, it's Chili, you better call me back. I'm tired of your bullshit. I told you I'm pregnant and it's yours and you know it. Now, you need to step up, I can't keep avoiding Kenisha's calls. You need to be a man and tell her, 'cause I'm not getting rid of this one like last time. I'm on my way over so you better be your ass home 'cause we need to talk now." It was obvious that she was excited and angry, but her words were crystal clear this time as she slammed the phone down.

I sat there, stunned. I swear I couldn't believe what I'd just heard, LaVon, my boyfriend, and Chili, my girl. Even rolling the names around in my head sounded strange. Then questions started pouring in. Where was I when all this was going on? Who else knew about them? When did this start? What she mean that she wasn't getting rid of this one like last time? Was Chili pregnant by LaVon before? That was how LaVon found me when he walked back in with a huge glass of water.

"A'ight, here's your water, let's do this." He put the glass down on the dresser, slapped his hands together, licked his lips, then walked over to the bed where I was still sitting. "What's wrong with you now?" he asked, seeing the expression on my face, I guess.

"What's wrong with me? What's wrong with everybody? Can't anybody tell me the truth?"

"What?" he asked.

"You should answer your phone sometimes, LaVon."

"Why?"

"It was Chili, she's on her way over here now."

"Ahh, shit, man, that skank is crazy, acting like I owe her something, like she own me. She's whacked. Don't listen to her, she's...hey, where you going, girl?" he asked, obviously surprised for some reason by my standing and leaving.

"I told you, you have company coming," I said.

"Come on, baby, she don't mean nothing to me, you know I love you, Kenisha. She was just putting out. You know what I mean, a man has needs and you wasn't supplying."

I chuckled. Of all the people who'd professed to love me in the past few weeks, his was by far the weakest. "Yeah, baby, I know you do, but you *needs* to get your business straight," I said as I walked past him.

"Aw, see, you wrong. We supposed to be doing this…"

I swung around to him. "Wait a minute, I'm wrong? One of my so-called best friends is on her way over to talk to you about your baby together and I'm wrong?"

"I told you, it ain't even about that, she's whacked. You know Chili, she'll sleep with anybody."

"Yeah, apparently." I turned and kept walking.

"I bet it ain't even mine," he said, following me down the stairs.

"You see, that was the point, LaVon, the possibility that it could be yours is the point of all this."

"What?"

"See ya." I went to the door just as the bell rang.

"Wait a minute," he said. I didn't. I grabbed the knob and swung the front door open wide. I must have stunned Chili, 'cause she just about jumped out of her skin. She looked up, then smiled, then panicked.

"Oh, shit, Kenisha, girl, I can explain, it's not what you think, I swear, I mean…" LaVon was still whining and begging behind me.

"Hey, girl," I said, playing off like I didn't know anything, "what are you doing here?" I asked.

Chili looked at me, then at LaVon standing behind me.

"Hey, girl," she said. "I thought I saw you coming in here. How you doing? I've been trying to find you for a couple of days."

"Really?" I said, looking at her, knowing she was lying.

"What," she asked, "you don't believe me?"

"I heard your message, Chili," I said, walking past her.

"Kenisha, it's not what you think…" she started.

"Kenisha, wait, wait, girl," LaVon called after me, brushing past Chili to catch up with me. "Wait a minute, girl. I was going to tell you, honest, but I thought your girls told you already and that you was cool with it."

"What, what girls?"

"Diamond and Jalisa knew."

"They knew," I said.

"They both knew?" Chili asked.

"Yeah, what, they ain't tell you, you need to step up to them, they was wrong for not saying anything."

"Shut up, don't even think about trying to turn this around on somebody else, you were wrong and you know it."

"But, but, but…"

I whipped around. "But what, LaVon, but what? Tell me, no, let me guess, you forgot, no, you were gonna call me, no, how about this one, you weren't man enough?"

"Look, it's not like, we wasn't all that tight anyway. You was holding out, so…"

"How could you do this to me, to us?"

"It ain't mean nothing, baby, believe me."

"Excuse me," Chili said indignantly, "what do you mean it ain't mean nothing?"

"See what I'm telling you, she whacked, it ain't even my baby. She was screwing, like, four other guys."

"It's your baby, asshole. I'm three months' pregnant and it's yours and you know it. It was the night a few weeks before my sixteenth birthday party," she said, stepping up quickly to him.

"Shut up, ain't nobody talking to you and if you think you riding me to the NBA, you're crazy..." he said.

"I don't want your little NBA change, my *papi* can buy and sell your ass..." she snapped back.

I turned and took one last look at them, glad at least that I was out of it. I turned back around and walked home. By the time I got there, I saw my dad's car parked out front. I was surprised to see it, because it was still early and he never came home early before, when it was just me and Mom.

I was just about to walk in the front door when I heard yelling coming from the back, so I walked around the side and found my dad and Courtney arguing. Apparently she was pissed 'cause she'd found out that he was stepping out on her. All I could do was smile. Some things never change.

"Fine, there she is, you talk to her," Courtney said.

My dad turned. "Are you all right?" he asked, acting all concerned.

"Yes, fine, why?" I said.

"You left the office suddenly, I called here and you weren't here, where did you go?"

"I went to Grandmom's house and then to Freeman."

"You're gonna have to start accounting for your whereabouts. I want to know where you are every minute of the day. You can't just walk in and out of here like this."

I wanted to laugh at his so-called parental rampage, but I didn't. "I need to talk to you," I said.

"That's gonna have to wait," Courtney said, "I made an early dinner and it's ready now." She turned to her kids in the pool. "I told y'all to get out of there ten minutes ago, didn't I? Now, come on, get out of there now."

"I'm not hungry," I said.

"You need to eat," my dad said.

"I ate at my grandmom's house."

"Fine," Courtney said to me, then turned back to her kids. "Junior, Jason, come on, let's go inside, it's time to eat. Get out of the pool now."

"Aw, do we have to?" the oldest moaned, soaking wet from playing in the pool. "I don't want to eat your food, it's nasty. I want pizza."

"Yeah, pizza, pizza, pizza, pizza…" the little one began, and so started the usual nerve-racking chanting. "Pizza, pizza, pizza…"

"No pizza, so get out of there now," she said to them, then turned to me. "By the way, Kenisha, it cost two hundred and fifty dollars to get the pool cleaned and have the chemicals added."

I glanced over and nodded. "They did a good job."

"You see, you see. This is what I have to put up with, and I'm sick and tired of it. We could have saved damn near three hundred dollars if she had done what I told her."

"Shut up, Courtney," I said.

"You gonna let her talk to me like that? Get out of that pool now," she said to the boys.

"Pizza, pizza, pizza, pizza…"

"Kenisha, apologize, now," my dad said firmly.

"Fine, I'm sorry that I just found out that Jade is my sister and that my father knew and didn't tell me."

My dad's face froze. *Priceless*.

"What kind of apology was that?" Courtney asked.

I didn't say anything, I just stared at my dad.

"Your grandmother told you."

"She shouldn't have had to. But no, she didn't, Jade told me. Why didn't you?"

"Pizza, pizza, pizza, pizza…"

"What is she talking about?" Courtney asked, then screamed to them about getting out of the pool again.

"I'm talking about the fact that I have an older sister, Jade, and for some reason I assumed that she was my cousin."

"What?" Courtney asked, looking at my father. "Jade is Kenisha's sister? You told me that she was her cousin. Well, I hope she's not moving in here, too. Come on, y'all, let's eat. Get out that water, now." She walked away, grabbed up towels and wrapped them around the kids, then marched the kids to the back door.

"We can talk over dinner," my dad said.

"No, thanks."

"Well, just come inside, then."

"I'll wait here for you."

He nodded and went inside with the rest of his family.

I sat down on a lounge chair, pulled out my cell and called my girls.

It was funny, I couldn't live without my cell before, but in the past few days I hadn't even seen it. I had over fifty messages, but I decided to call Jalisa and Diamond first. I needed to find out when our friendship had broken down. I got them into a three-way conversation.

"Hey," I said evenly when they connected. They both started talking at once.

"Where you been, are you all right, where are you, we been calling you for days, we were worried when nobody heard from you, how's you grandmother, are you in Virginia or in D.C., we need to talk to you, where are you now?"

"I'm at my dad and his girlfriend's house."

"What?" they both said.

"My dad moved his girlfriend into our old house. They have two kids together and another one on the way."

"What?" Diamond repeated.

"Are you serious?" Jalisa said.

"Yeah, I'm serious," I said.

"But he's married to your mom," Jalisa said.

"No, he's a widow now," Diamond stated.

"All this was before my mom died. We moved out so that he could move her in," I said.

"How could that happen?" Diamond asked.

"They were divorcing, right?" Jalisa said.

"No, they were never married, I didn't know until we moved to D.C."

The line was quiet for a brief moment as we all processed the information. "We got something to tell you," Jalisa said slowly.

"We know you gonna be pissed off, but you're gonna find out anyway," Diamond added, "so..."

"But we didn't know how to tell you before," Jalisa added.

"Just tell her," Diamond said to Jalisa.

"Chili's pregnant again," Jalisa said.

"What is this, number two or three?" I asked absently.

"There's more, it's about the father..." Diamond began, "...we heard that it was LaVon."

"Y'all knew they were sleeping together, but nobody thought I might want to know," I said angrily. They didn't say anything. "Y'all ain't tell me. Why, y'all supposed to be my girls?"

"How were we supposed to tell you that?" Jalisa said.

"'Cause you were so happy with LaVon, talking about the NBA and everything and how large y'all were gonna be."

"So y'all were jealous of us."

"No," they both said firmly, ending that thought. "We were happy for you until we found out..."

"We didn't know how to tell you," Jalisa continued, "and you were already pissed at Diamond 'cause Chili lied to you, trying to hide the fact that she was..."

"Did you see them together?" I asked.

"I did," Diamond said, "right before her birthday I saw them going into his house, kissing. At first I thought it was you and I was gonna call out, but then..."

"Me, too," Jalisa said slowly. "I was hanging out in the projection booth and they came in separately but sat together and started making out in the back."

"Is that all?" I asked, expecting more.

"But her baby might not even be his."

"Yeah, you know how Chili is."

"It is his," I said.

"You already heard?" they both asked.

"Yeah, by accident, I was over LaVon's house earlier when she left a message for him. I heard it."

"Are you okay?" they asked.

"Are you kidding?"

"So how far along is she, I wonder?"

"She said three months, and she's gonna have it this time."

"So you can figure that they must have been together when you and LaVon were, I mean, what I'm saying is…"

"Don't even trip about that. I guess I knew before that he was getting with somebody else, that was when Chili told me that it was you, Diamond, but whatever."

"So you pissed off at us, right?"

"Yeah, we supposed to be girls, we supposed to have each other's back, and y'all knew but didn't even say anything to me. That was wrong." The line went silent again and suddenly I felt so tired.

"So what now?" Jalisa asked.

"I guess we're not girls anymore," Diamond said.

I looked up and saw my dad standing at the back door. I guess it was time to get that drama over with next.

"I gotta go," I said, and hung up, but just as I closed my cell it rang.

"Hey, I was gonna call you," LaVon said.

"No, you weren't."

"See, all that stuff before, that was nothing, don't even think about that crazy stuff. Chili just messing up."

"Yeah, I bet."

"Listen, we need to talk. I know I was wrong and all when we was together at you grandmother's house, I must have been tripping or something. But I'm sorry. I get it. We can slow down, a'ight."

"That's not even necessary anymore," I told him.

"So now you pissed off, right?"

"Yeah, something like that."

"A'ight, so let me explain, then…"

"You know what, I'm busy right now, LaVon, later."

I hung up, then looked up and saw my father coming outside toward me. He sat down next to me.

"Jade is my sister," I said. He didn't answer. "Did you hear me, I said that Jade is my sister."

"She's your half sister, yes."

"So why didn't I know?"

"You were too young."

"I'm fifteen years old."

"You were too young at the time, it would have been confusing. She lived with your grandmother, it was better that way."

"Better for who? It's the twenty-first century, not 1910. Things have relaxed in family morality. There are such things as blended families. What was so confusing?"

"My mother was married before she married my father. She had a son, my half brother, and he was white like her. Older, bigger, he teased me mercilessly and she never said a word, just to be a big boy and stop complaining. So I did. Every time my father left the house to go to work, I was mentally abused by him. Then my dad left her, and after that, my brother could do no wrong. As the youngest I was scorned, belittled, ridiculed, teased and mocked. My father left and they took it out on me. The firstborn was her favorite, and I didn't want that for you. And as far as Jade was concerned, what's done is done."

"But all that had nothing to do with me and Jade."

"I didn't want that for you, I was protecting you. Your mother loved Jade…"

"Yes, she did, and she loved me, too, I knew that, I know that. I felt it, I feel it even now. She's dead and I still feel her love around me. She never would have done that to me, to us. You should have trusted her."

"I couldn't take that chance."

"Couldn't you see it broke her heart to separate us, the guilt, the pain, it killed her inside. No wonder she couldn't sleep and took the pills. And you didn't marry her, why, because your own parents broke up and your father left you in that mess."

He started crying, whimpering like a baby. I reached out to him and held him. "She was so perfect, my Barbie doll. I loved her so much, but she changed, she changed… the pills and everything, she didn't talk to me, she should have told me…"

"I lost out on having a sister and you lost out on having a wife."

He sat up and leaned away. "What's done is done." He glanced at the back door. "I have a new family now."

"Is that all you have to say? Mom's dead and all you

have to say is what's done is done. I guess your mother was right, I should be a big girl and stop complaining, right? Except only this time you're keeping the youngest and throwing me away."

CHAPTER 20

Pushing Pause

"I tried to shake off the craziness. But I saw myself going down the path of self-destruction. Maybe Mom was right all along, we are who we are, unchanged by it all, following one path."

—*myspace.com*

PUSHed out, kicked out, betrayed, ignored...

Enough.

I went back to my grandmother's house. There was nobody there, so I just went upstairs. I had been running around all day and I was tired, plus I hadn't really slept in I don't know how long. All I wanted was to make all this go away, make it like it was before, but I knew I couldn't.

Everything and everyone was gone.

Mom, Dad, LaVon, my friends, there was no one I could depend on anymore. I was alone for the first time in my life. I had nothing, no home, no boyfriend, no friends and no family. I sat on the bed just staring across the room.

There were still a few boxes that I'd never unpacked sitting in the corner of my room. One was the box my mother had asked me to take to her room the first day we got there. I had forgotten all about it. So since it didn't matter anymore, I got up and sat it on the bed and opened it up and started going through it.

Inside were large manila envelopes labeled James, Barbra, Kenisha and Jade. I pulled them out and set them aside. The bottom of the box was filled with pill bottles.

I pulled each one out and stared at the labels, prescriptions from a lot of different doctors. They had refill dates for the next six months. How could she have done this to herself, to me? The question hung in the air. It would never be answered.

I was so tired.

I opened the first bottle and poured out the tiny pills in the palm of my hand. They looked so small and innocent like little candy buttons. I opened the second bottle. Baby blue and larger. Then the third bottle with pink ones, and the fourth one contained pale octagons. The last one was the largest, but some of them had already been broken in half.

I looked at them in my hand, about eighty or ninety.

I felt alone and empty and tempted.

"You're not gonna do anything stupid, are you?"

I looked up and saw Jade standing in my doorway. She was staring at me, expecting an answer. I didn't feel like talking, so I just ignored her. "'Cause if you are, I'd like to know now. Surprises just aren't what they used to be."

I looked down at my hand.

"What's going on?" somebody asked behind her.

I heard a man's voice and I looked up again. There was someone standing behind Jade, her mysterious boyfriend, I assumed. I didn't care, I looked back at my hand.

"Hey, little sister, what you got there?" he asked, coming into the room.

"This is Kenisha, Ty."

"So this is Kenisha. How you doing?"

"If you've come to see the show, just sit down and shut up," I said, pouring more pills into the palm of my hand.

"Put them away," Jade ordered firmly.

"Oh, now you gonna come off with sisterly concern, please. You should be the last person to want to stop me. Just think, no more Kenisha."

She walked over and sat on my bed. I still didn't look up at her. "True, I'd have the third floor to myself again and I wouldn't have to listen to your loud snoring anymore." She picked up a few of the bottles and read the labels. "For depression. For pain relief. For anxiety. For stress. For congestion. For motion sickness and for nothing at all. You have all these symptoms?" she asked.

"Yeah, I have all that."

"So what are you gonna do, Kenisha?"

"Do you know what happened?" I asked, looking at her.

She looked at me strangely. "With Mom and your dad, his name was Jaden, right?"

"What are you talking about?"

"I know something happened, I just don't know what."

"My father died. He was hit by a drunk driver."

"Was Mom there?"

"He pushed her out of the way but couldn't move fast enough to save himself. So he was killed instead of her."

"He risked his life to save her."

"Yes."

"That was real love."

"Yeah, I think it was, too," she said.

"Then what?" I asked.

"I was only three years old, Kenisha, I don't really remember."

"But you know what happened though. Mom told you."

"Mom got over it and married your dad."

"No, she didn't. Jade, tell me the truth, please, for once can someone please treat me like a person and tell me the truth?"

"Now that you're acting like a person and not like a snobbish brat...the truth," she said. I nodded, steeling myself for whatever. "Mom and my father met in college freshman year. He was seventeen, she was sixteen. After they had me they stayed together and planned to finish college, then get married. But something happened, they got into an argument about it or something and she ran out. He followed her. She didn't see the car coming, he did. He pushed her out of the way."

"Then she met my dad?" I asked.

"No, the argument was about James."

"Mom was seeing my dad while she was with your father, right?" I asked.

She nodded. "Your dad had money and was popular because he was a former football player. She was working for his company part-time, and I guess they hooked up."

"Your dad died, and Mom just went off with my dad."

She nodded. "How come you didn't come with her?"

She smirked. "I did at first, I even lived at the house. We shared a bedroom. Then I had to leave, I don't really know why. But she snuck me over to the house almost every day. And then James found out and told her that it was either him or me. She chose him."

"How did he find out?"

"I don't know."

"Yes, you do," I said, knowing that she was lying, "I told him, didn't I? I remember now. We fought about the doll and I told my dad you took my doll from me." Jade didn't say anything. "That was when you stopped coming over, I remember now." She stood up to leave. "Wait," I said, "it was me, right, I told my dad about you, didn't I? It was me that got you kicked out and made Mom choose."

"You were, like, three years old. You were a kid just talking. It was nobody's fault."

"Jade, I'm so sorry, really."

"Kenisha, whatever."

"No, look what I did to you, I messed up your life, I'm sorry. You had to come live here with Grandmom and I stayed in Virginia. I'm sorry."

"I'm not," she said, then smiled. "You know, I used to be so jealous of you. You had everything I wanted. Mom and a father and a big house and money. But then you were so mean about it. You walked in here like some kind of diva, like everything and everybody was beneath you. But I knew that you were gonna have to wake up one day, just like Mom did, and realize that the money wasn't worth it. She sacrificed her dream, her heart, for money and you were doing the same thing. That was why she stayed on your case."

"Jade, I'm so sorry I…" I reached out and took her hand. She didn't pull away this time, and she didn't go limp, she held tight and it was like I'd found a lifeline to hold on to.

"It's okay, we're good. I don't envy you anymore. I'm not jealous or angry. That was over a long time ago. Besides, I might need a kidney one day."

"Damn," Ty said quietly, more to himself then to us.

We both looked up. "Ty, I forgot you were still standing there," Jade said.

"OMG, you're Tyrece Grant," I said.

"Kenisha, this is Tyrece, my fiancé." She held out her hand and produced a serious rock on her third finger.

"Hey, little sister, I just got back in the country, I'm sorry about Barbra. She was cool, real cool," he said.

"You're engaged to *him?*" I asked.

"Yeah."

"Oh—my—God."

Jade turned to Tyrece. "You ready to go?"

"Yeah, sure, but why don't we flush these, unless, of course, the show is still on," he said.

We started picking up the pills, then Jade took them all and flushed them down the toilet. "Is that it?" she asked when she came back.

"Yeah, that's it," I said. Then for some reason I started crying and I couldn't stop. Tyrece went downstairs and got me a glass of water, then he got me an ice pack 'cause

I was burning up, then he went to tell my grandmother, who sent word that I'd be okay now. I just kept crying, for my mom, my dad, for Jade, for my grandmother, for my girls, but mostly for me.

I'd lost everything I'd tried to hold on to, but I could tell that I was kind of starting over. I just wasn't sure I was ready.

CHAPTER 21

Pushing Play—The Beginning

"I thought the puzzle of me was already put together, but it wasn't. Missing, mislaid, torn, damaged, destroyed... picking up the scattered pieces of my life, I see now how the choices we make have consequences."

—*myspace.com*

After Jade and Tyrece left to take her things back to the dorm, I fell asleep and dreamed about my mother. I didn't really remember the dream just that I dreamed about her and it made me feel good. I slept the rest of the evening, that night and most of the next morning. I finally got up around ten. I was hot even though the air conditioner had been on.

I showered and got dressed, then went downstairs. The first thing I heard was the lawn mower outside. I smiled. I went out the back door expecting to see lawn mower guy, but it was somebody else. I saw my grandmother in her garden. I went over to her. "Morning, Grandmom."

"Good morning, did you sleep well?"

"Yes, I passed out, I was tired."

"Good, you needed your rest."

I looked around, still curious. "Do you need some help with that?"

"Sure, just pinch off the spent flowers and toss them in the basket."

I started doing that, following her. "Um, where's the other guy?"

"What other guy?"

"The guy that used to cut your grass."

"Terrence, Terrence Butler, from next door. He's gone."

"Gone, where? I mean, like, did he get in trouble again or something?"

"Trouble? What, no. Classes started for him."

"I thought he dropped out of high school."

"Dropped out, no, you must still be tired. He graduated last semester and got a scholarship. He's a freshman at Howard this fall."

"How old is he?"

"Seventeen, if I'm not mistaken."

"But I thought— Never mind," I said, then followed her around, snipping the spent flowers as she schooled me on the names and scents in her herb garden. We were out there a while, then she went back inside and left me to plant a tray of flowers while she got us something to drink.

"Hey."

I turned around and saw Diamond and Jalisa coming down the back steps to stand behind me. "Hey." I stood up.

"We're sorry. We talked and we don't want..."

"I know, me, neither. I'm sorry, too, I was acting all crazy. I don't care about LaVon and Chili and all that. They deserve each other. So, are we girls again?" We smiled and hugged each other, then they laughed at me wearing my grandmother's garden hat to keep out the bright sun.

"That's a new look for you," Diamond said.

"You like?" I asked.

"I do, where do we get one?" Jalisa added.

We joked, then turned when someone cleared their throat, getting our attention.

Lawn mower guy stood there looking at us.

"Hey," I said. "I wondered what happened to you."

"I had to do something." He smiled, showing his dimple.

"Yeah, my grandmother told me. You're a freshman at Howard, not bad."

"Yeah, a brother has skills."

"Um, these are my girls, Jalisa and Diamond, and this is Terrence Butler, he lives next door."

They greeted each other. "I didn't know you knew my name, Kenisha. You always call me lawn mower guy."

"I didn't, my grandmother just told me."

Diamond and Jalisa looked at each other. "Umm, listen, we're gonna go now, Kenisha…"

"Yeah, we'll call you later, after dance class."

"Oh, right, dance class," I said. "I'm going, too."

"But don't you want to stay and talk and…" Jalisa said.

"…hang out or something?" Diamond finished.

"Nah," I said, looking at Terrence. "He'll be here when I get back, right?"

He nodded slowly, flashing that dimple. I walked over and kissed him sweetly.

"We'll meet you out front," Jalisa said as she and Diamond started giggling and hurrying around the side of the house.

"So you gonna be here for me when I get back?" I asked, holding on to him.

"Yeah, I can do that," he said, then kissed me back.

A few minutes later I grabbed my dance bag and hurried downstairs. My grandmother and Terrence were on the front porch, talking.

"See you later, Grandmom, I'll be home right after dance class."

"All right, I'll cook your favorite."

"Thanks, Grandmom, I love you."

"I love you, too, Kenisha."

"See ya, shorty," Terrence said.

"See ya, lawn mower guy."

I caught up with Jalisa and Diamond and we decided to walk instead of taking Diamond's car. "All right, ladies, check, have I got something to tell you…"

We talked and walked and squealed and joked and laughed all the way there. On the way I looked around my new neighborhood. It wasn't that bad. Kids still played, guys still hung out and trees still grew. I had my friends, a new sister, my grandmother and dance. Who would want anything more?

Oh, and I also had lawn mower guy.